# BRIAN . _ . ...

# THE BILLIARD-ROOM MYSTERY

With an introduction by
Steve Barge

DEAN STREET PRESS

# INTRODUCTION

"I believe that the primary function of the mystery story is to entertain; to stimulate the imagination and even, at times, to supply humour. But it pleases the connoisseur most when it presents – and reveals – genuine mystery. To reach its full height, it has to offer an intellectual problem for the reader to consider, measure and solve."

THUS WROTE Brian Flynn in the *Crime Book Magazine* in 1948, setting out his ethos on writing detective fiction. At that point in his career, Flynn had published thirty-six mystery novels, beginning with *The Billiard-Room Mystery* in 1927 – he went on, before his death in 1958, to write twenty-one more, three under the pseudonym Charles Wogan. So how is it that the general reading populace – indeed, even some of the most ardent collectors of mystery fiction – were until recently unaware of his existence? The reputation of writers such as John Rhode survived their work being out of print, so what made Flynn and his books vanish so completely?

There are many factors that could have contributed to Flynn's disappearance. For reasons unknown, he was not a member of either The Detection Club or the Crime Writers' Association, two of the best ways for a writer to network with others. As such, his work never appeared in the various collaborations that those groups published. The occasional short story in such a collection can be a way of maintaining awareness of an author's name, but it seems that Brian Flynn wrote no short stories at all, something rare amongst crime writers.

There are a few mentions of him in various studies of the genre over the years. Sutherland Scott, in *Blood in Their Ink* (1953), states that Flynn, who was still writing at the time, "has long been popular". He goes on to praise *The Mystery of the Peacock's Eye* (1928) as containing "one of the ablest pieces of misdirection one could wish to meet". Anyone reading that particular review who feels like picking up the novel – out now from Dean Street Press – should stop reading at that point, as later in the book, Scott proceeds to casually spoil the ending, although as if he assumes that everyone will have read the novel already.

It is a later review, though, that may have done much to end – temporarily, I hope – Flynn's popularity.

> "Straight tripe and savorless. It is doubtful, on the evidence, if any of his others would be different."

Thus wrote Jacques Barzun and Wendell Hertig Taylor in their celebrated work, *A Catalog of Crime* (1971). The book was an ambitious attempt to collate and review every crime fiction author, past and present. They presented brief reviews of some titles, a bibliography of some authors and a short biography of others. It is by no means complete – E & M.A. Radford had written thirty-six novels at this point in time but garner no mention – but it might have helped Flynn's reputation if he too had been overlooked. Instead one of the contributors picked up *Conspiracy at Angel* (1947), the thirty-second Anthony Bathurst title. I believe that title has a number of things to enjoy about it, but as a mystery, it doesn't match the quality of the majority of Flynn's output. Dismissing a writer's entire work on the basis of a single volume is questionable, but with the amount of crime writers they were trying to catalogue, one can, just about, understand the decision. But that decision meant that they missed out on a large number of truly entertaining mysteries that fully embrace the spirit of the Golden Age of Detection, and, moreover, many readers using the book as a reference work may have missed out as well.

So who was Brian Flynn? Born in 1885 in Leyton, Essex, Flynn won a scholarship to the City Of London School, and while he went into the civil service (ranking fourth in the whole country on the entrance examination) rather than go to university, the classical education that he received there clearly stayed with him. Protracted bouts of rheumatic fever prevented him fighting in the Great War, but instead he served as a Special Constable on the Home Front – one particular job involved warning the populace about Zeppelin raids armed only with a bicycle, a whistle and a placard reading "TAKE COVER". Flynn worked for the local government while teaching "Accountancy, Languages, Maths and Elocution to men, women, boys and girls" in the evening, and acting as part of the Trevalyan Players in his spare time.

It was a seaside family holiday that inspired him to turn his hand to writing. He asked his librarian to supply him a collection of mystery novels for "deck-chair reading" only to find himself disappointed. In his own words, they were "mediocre in the extreme." There is no record of what those books were, unfortunately, but on arriving home, the following conversation, again in Brian's own words, occurred:

> "ME (unpacking the books): If I couldn't write better stuff than any of these, I'd eat my own hat.
>
> Mrs ME (after the manner of women and particularly after the manner of wives): It's a great pity you don't do a bit more and talk a bit less.
>
> The shaft struck home. I accepted the challenge, laboured like the mountain and produced *The Billiard-Room Mystery*."

"Mrs ME", or Edith as most people referred to her, deserves our gratitude. While there were some delays with that first book, including Edith finding the neglected half-finished manuscript in a drawer where it had been "resting" for six months, and a protracted period finding a publisher, it was eventually released in 1927 by John Hamilton in the UK and Macrae Smith in the U.S. According to Flynn, John Hamilton asked for five more, but in fact they only published five in total, all as part of the Sundial Mystery Library imprint. Starting with *The Five Red Fingers* (1929), Flynn was published by John Long, who would go on to publish all of his remaining novels, bar his single non-series title, *Tragedy At Trinket* (1934). About ten of his early books were reprinted in the US before the war, either by Macrae Smith, Grosset & Dunlap or Mill, and a few titles also appeared in France, Denmark, Germany and Sweden, but the majority of his output only saw print in the United Kingdom. Some titles were reprinted during his lifetime – the John Long Four-Square Thrillers paperback range featured some Flynn titles, for example – but John Long's primary focus was the library market, and some titles had relatively low print runs. Currently, the majority of Flynn's work, in particular that only published in the U.K., is extremely rare – not just expensive, but seemingly non-existent even in the second-hand book market.

In the aforementioned article, Flynn states that the tales of Sherlock Holmes were a primary inspiration for his writing, having read them at a young age. A conversation in *The Billiard-Room Mystery* hints at other influences on his writing style. A character, presumably voicing Flynn's own thoughts, states that he is a fan of "the pre-war Holmes". When pushed further, he states that:

> "Mason's M. Hanaud, Bentley's Trent, Milne's Mr Gillingham and to a lesser extent, Agatha Christie's M. Poirot are all excellent in their way, but oh! – the many dozens that aren't."

He goes on to acknowledge the strengths of Bernard Capes' "Baron" from *The Mystery of The Skeleton Key* and H.C. Bailey's Reggie Fortune, but refuses to accept Chesterton's Father Brown.

> "He's entirely too Chestertonian. He deduces that the dustman was the murderer because of the shape of the piece that had been cut from the apple-pie."

Perhaps this might be the reason that the invitation to join the Detection Club never arrived . . .

Flynn created a sleuth that shared a number of traits with Holmes, but was hardly a carbon-copy. Enter Anthony Bathurst, a polymath and gentleman sleuth, a man of contradictions whose background is never made clear to the reader. He clearly has money, as he has his own rooms in London with a pair of servants on call and went to public school (Uppingham) and university (Oxford). He is a follower of all things that fall under the banner of sport, in particular horse racing and cricket, the latter being a sport that he could, allegedly, have represented England at. He is also a bit of a show-off, littering his speech (at times) with classical quotes, the obscurer the better, provided by the copies of the *Oxford Dictionary of Quotations* and *Brewer's Dictionary of Phrase & Fable* that Flynn kept by his writing desk, although Bathurst generally restrains himself to only doing this with people who would appreciate it or to annoy the local constabulary. He is fond of amateur dramatics (as was Flynn, a well-regarded amateur thespian who appeared in at least one self-penned play, *Blue Murder*), having been a member of OUDS, the Oxford University Dramatic Society. Like Holmes, Bathurst isn't averse to the occasional disguise, and as with Watson and Holmes, sometimes even his close allies don't recognise him. General information about his background is light on the ground. His parents were Irish, but he doesn't have an accent – see *The Spiked Lion* (1933) – and his eyes are grey. We learn in *The Orange Axe* that he doesn't pursue romantic relationships due to a bad experience in his first romance. That doesn't remain the case throughout the series – he falls head over heels in love in *Fear and Trembling*, for example – but in this opening tranche of titles, we don't see Anthony distracted by the fairer sex, not even one who will only entertain gentlemen who can beat her at golf!

Unlike a number of the Holmes' stories, Flynn's Bathurst tales are all fairly clued mysteries, perhaps a nod to his admiration of Christie, but first and foremost, Flynn was out to entertain the reader. The problems posed to Bathurst have a flair about them – the simultaneous murders, miles apart, in *The Case of the Black Twenty-Two* (1928) for example, or the scheme to draw lots to commit masked murder in *The Orange Axe* – and there is a momentum to the narrative. Some mystery writers have trouble with the pace slowing between the reveal of the problem and the reveal of the murderer, but Flynn's books sidestep that, with Bathurst's investigations never seeming to sag. He writes with a wit and intellect that can make even the most prosaic of interviews with suspects enjoyable to read about, and usually provides an action-packed finale before the murderer is finally revealed. Some of those revelations, I think it is fair to say, are surprises that can rank with some of the best in crime fiction.

We are fortunate that we can finally reintroduce Brian Flynn and Anthony Lotherington Bathurst to the many fans of classic crime fiction out there.

## *The Billiard-Room Mystery* (1927)

*"I've always been attracted by affairs of this nature, sir, little thinking that one day I should be swept into one. Would you be good enough to give me carte blanche as it were, to do a little investigating off my own bat?"*

IF YOU are going to murder someone in a grand country house, it's always best to do it in one of the grandest rooms in the house, one of those rooms that is unique to the homes of the gentry. And if the library has already been taken, the billiard room would be the next best thing.

Billiards is one of those games that crossed all classes of the British populace. It dates back to the 15th century, although that version was played on a lawn akin to croquet. It soon became an indoor table-based game, with the playing surface coloured green in memory of its origins, and from the mid-nineteenth century, the table had taken its current form. The general populace would play in billiard halls, but the great and the good might have their own private billiard room – a vast room devoted entirely to the one game, given the size of the table and the amount of space needed around it. Not to mention the room needed for a "handy seat on either side of the table . . . for the player who happens to be out of play" and a "smoker's cabinet and a small cabinet for drinks", as suggested by *The House Beautiful and Useful* (1911). Note the latter is apparently unnecessary if you place the room near to the butler's pantry . . .

When Flynn was writing the book, snooker, a more colourful version of the game that was played on the same table, was in the ascendance, but in Considine Manor, the location of *The Billiard-Room Mystery*, the billiard room was still the place for the gentlemen to retire to after dinner. Or to get murdered in . . .

When Flynn set out to write his first novel, he was determined to improve on those unnamed novels that he had recently read, and *The Billiard-Room Mystery* makes clear his intentions. First and foremost is entertainment. The murder is suitably odd, with a body found both strangled with his own shoelace and stabbed with an antique Venetian dagger, a murder that happens as the same time as a jewellery theft. The setting would be familiar to those readers who devour detective fiction. The country house party, which Flynn would return to at least once in his first ten books, was already becoming a cliché, even in 1927, but it put Flynn in a genre that he could write about with confidence. At a guess, that confidence came from his own reading, as he would not have attended many such events himself. There is more than a hint of Conan Doyle, with one of the guests, Bill Cunningham, narrating the adventure, while making the occasional Holmesian reference, but unlike Holmes, there is a surfeit of clues for the reader to try and interpret.

The cross-section of guests will also be familiar. The lord and lady of the manor, their married daughter, their unmarried son, their unmarried daughter who may or may not have been wooed by the victim, a servant or two with dubious intentions, a few cricketers of varying persuasions and one would-be sleuth all combine to form the cast of characters that one would expect to find. As one might expect, there is the odd eccentricity amongst their character traits, although this one is, I think, unique. Mary Considine, the unmarried daughter of the family, has strict conditions on whether she will step out with a young man or not. He has to beat her at cricket and a round of golf. While that comes across as particularly odd, it does lend itself to an exciting sequence where Bill, the narrator, tries his hand at romance.

The tone is a generally light one. As is often the case in Golden Age detective fiction, no one seems to be particularly upset about the murder – luckily the body didn't bleed much, so the billiard table is undamaged. Lord Considine does opine at one point about the difficulty of attracting people to subsequent Cricket Weeks in case they get murdered, but doesn't seem especially bothered apart from that. Bathurst treats the investigation as a bit of a game, playing off against Inspector Baddeley by sharing some, but not all, of his discoveries and theories. To be fair to him, Baddeley does the same, but as he is an actual policeman rather than an inexperienced amateur, that's probably fair.

Reviews of the book at the time were very positive. The *Nottingham Herald* refers to it as "a classic of its type", while the *Bystander* states it is "a very good yarn, I think, off the usual lines and most ingeniously contrived".

Reprinted now for the first time in over ninety years, *The Billiard-Room Mystery* is a strong debut for an author who has been overlooked for far too long.

Steve Barge

# CHAPTER I
# MR. BATHURST AS AN AID
# TO MEMORY

SEEING BATHURST this evening, after a lapse of eight years, has given me a most insistent inclination to set down, for the first time, the real facts of that *cause célèbre*, that was called by the Press at the time, the "Billiard Room Mystery." Considering the length of the interval, and regarding the whole affair from every possible point of view, it is sufficiently plain to me that an authentic history of the case can harm nobody and can prejudice no interests. I therefore succumb to the temptation, serenely confident that, no matter what shortcomings there may be in the telling, the affair itself as a whole, is entitled to rank as one of the most baffling in the annals of criminology.

Inasmuch as I was a member of the audience to-night at a private theatrical performance and Anthony Bathurst was playing lead for the company (amateur of course) that was entertaining us, I had no opportunity for conversation with him, but I am certain that had I had this opportunity, I should have found that his brain had lost none of its cunning and that his uncanny gifts for deduction, inference, and intuition, were unimpaired. These powers allied to a masterly memory for detail and to an unusual athleticism of body, separated him from the majority—wherever he was, he always counted—one acknowledged instinctively his mental supremacy—he was a personality always and everywhere. A tall, lithe body with that poised balance of movement that betrays the able player of all ball games, his clean-cut, clean-shaven face carried a mobile, sensitive mouth and grey eyes. Remarkable eyes that seemed to apprehend and absorb at a sweep every detail about you that was worth apprehending. A man's man, and, at the same time, a ladies' man. For when he chose, he was hard to resist, I assure you. Such, eight years ago, was Anthony Lotherington Bathurst, and such had he promised to be from comparative immaturity, for he had been with me at Uppingham, and afterwards at Oxford.

Which latter fact goes to the prime reason of my being at Considine Manor in the last week of July of the year of the tragedy.

At Oxford we had both grown very pally with Jack Considine, eldest son of Sir Charles Considine, of Considine Manor, Sussex, and although Bathurst had to a certain extent fallen away from the closest relations of the friendship, Jack and I were bosom companions, and it became my custom each year, when the 'Varsity came down, to spend a week at Considine Manor, and to take part in Sir Charles' Cricket Week. For I was a fairly useful member, and had been on the fringe of the 'Varsity Eleven; indeed many excellent judges were of the opinion that Prescott, who had been given the last place, was an inferior man. But of that, more later.

Bathurst never took his 'Varsity cricket seriously enough. Had he done so he would probably have skippered England—he's the kind that distinguishes whatever he sets his hand to—but it was cricket that took me to Considine Manor, and it was cricket that took both Prescott and Bathurst—but not in the same direction.

Sir Charles that year was particularly anxious to have a good team—which got Prescott his invitation. An invitation that he had certainly not lingered over accepting. For he had met Mary Considine at Twickenham the previous autumn, and had improved upon that acquaintanceship at Lords' in the first week of July. Mary was the third and youngest child, Jack coming between her and her sister, Helen, who had married a Captain Arkwright—a big, bluff Dragoon. Now whatever Prescott's feelings may have been towards Mary, I had no idea then, what hers were to him. Decidedly, I have no idea now; I can only surmise. But Mary Considine with her birth, her breeding and her beauty was a peach of peaches. She had grace, she had charm, and a pair of heavy-lashed, Parma violet eyes that sent all a man's good resolutions to the four winds of heaven and to my mind at least, it was something like presumption on Prescott's part to lift his eyes to her. Still that was only my opinion. As I said, what encouragement he received I have little knowledge of.

\* \* \* \* \*

The Cricket Week passed off comparatively uneventfully. The first three one-day games—I forget whom against, except one against the "Incogs"—were relatively unimportant. That is, to Sir Charles! His *pièce de résistance* was always kept for the Thursday and Friday, the last two days of the week. Then came the hardy annual—Sir Charles Considine's Eleven, versus "The Uppingham Rovers." Prior to this last game I had failed lamentably, my bag being 3, 7 and a couple of balloons. Two of the days were wet and real cricket out of the question. Prescott had a lot of luck and got a couple of centuries and a 70 odd in four times. Which of course gave him a good conceit of himself.

"Bill," said Mary to me on the Thursday morning, "I do hope you see them all right to-day—Gerry Prescott's getting a bit of 'roll' on, charming man though he be."

I finished my fourth egg and remarked, "Thanks, Mary— I'll have a good try, but I don't seem able to do anything right lately—still my luck must turn before long. Thanks again." She slipped over to the sideboard and helped herself to some Kedgeree—smiled—and then replied, "I think it will—*to-day.*" The rest of the crowd then joined us—Jack, Gerry Prescott, Helen and Dick Arkwright, Sir Charles and Lady Considine, three boys from the 'Varsity, Tennant, Daventry and Robertson, and two Service men, friends of Arkwright, Major Hornby and Lieutenant Barker—the last five all pretty decent cricketers—the rest of the eleven being recruited from the Manor staff.

It was, I remember, a perfectly glorious summer morning. One's thoughts instinctively flew to the whirr of the mowing machine and a real plumb wicket. The insects hummed in the sun, and there was a murmur of bees that gave everybody a feeling that an English summer morning in Sussex could give anything in Creation a start and a beating.

"Toppin' mornin'—what?" said Prescott. "Feel like gettin' some more to-day, if we bat."

"You won't," said Dick Arkwright. "You'll field, and this big brute of a Bill can get rid of some of his disgraceful paunch.

He hasn't had much exercise all the week. Exceptin' of course walkin' back to the pavilion."

"Feeling funny, aren't you?" I sallied back. "And as for 'big brutes' and 'paunches,' neither you nor Prescott has a lot to telegraph home about."

Actually I was about a couple of inches taller than either of them and decidedly heavier.

"Anybody of the old crowd playing for the Rovers, Jack?" queried Helen.

"Don't know, haven't seen the team yet."

Daventry, I think, handed the *Sporting Life* to the two girls. They scanned the names.

"Only Toby Purkiss and Vernon Hurst that we know," from Mary. "What a pity."

"I am very keen on winning," boomed Sir Charles. "Very, very keen. We haven't beaten the Rovers for more years than I care to—ah—remember. I spoke seriously to Briggs this morning about it. And I may say, here and now, Tennant—Daventry—I trust without offence, that I viewed with some disfavour your late retirement last night. You were very late getting to bed. I am willing to concede that Auction Bridge has a fascination—"

"That's all right, Governor," said Jack. "They're just infants—stand anything. Think what a tough bird you were at their age."

"Perfectly true. I remember the night I—"

"As long as you can remember it, you can't have been so bad, sir," said Daventry.

Lady Considine smiled.

"Would you like me to stop Auction in the evening, till the week is over, dear?" she said. "You never seem to win anything."

"As a matter of fact, Marion—I have been most unusually successful; and I have no wish to—er—interfere with others' pleasure."

"Thanks, Father. For we don't all play cricket."

"No, Helen, that's so."

"Seems to me, Governor, it takes age and judgment to play really good Auction."

"Thank you, Arkwright. You have keen powers of observance."

The clock chimed ten.

"Gracious," said Mary, "I promised to help get the big marquee ready." She flew off. Very shortly the breakfast party withdrew entirely, the ladies to the selection of appropriate raiment, the men who were playing, to get ready.

I was late getting down to the field and had no sooner arrived than up came Sir Charles.

"Fielding, Bill!" He guessed right. "Know you're pleased!" he grinned.

"Of course—just what I expected! It'll rain in the night."

The first wicket put on a few runs and I was chatting to Robertson and Jack Considine while we were waiting for the next man.

"Good Lord," I heard from behind me.

I turned.

Strolling in, nonchalantly adjusting his left-hand glove, was the very last person I expected to see there—Anthony Bathurst.

"Bless you, Bill," he smiled. "Seeing you is a reward in itself."

"But I had no idea—"

"What on earth?" queried Jack.

"Tell you later," grinned Anthony; "Umpire, Middle and leg, if you please."

He didn't get a lot. But when we got into lunch he told us that Hurst had cried off from the game, developed measles or spotted fever or something, and he had been roped in, being handy. He was staying near Bramber and going on to Canterbury for the "Old Stagers." Angus McKinnel and Gerry Crookley were great chums of his, and as the entertainments of Canterbury Week were in their hands as usual, they had been only too glad for him to help them.

Everybody, of course, was delighted, for Considine Manor had heard much of Anthony Bathurst from both Jack and me.

Sir Charles immediately issued an invitation.

"Stay on, my dear fellow! I shall be charmed, I assure you. Stay till the Bank Holiday—then motor over."

"Thanks, I will. It's good of you." Anthony accepted the offer.

Thus, it was that the Friday evening saw Anthony still at Considine Manor, and the stage set for what happened subsequently. When I reached the drawing-room that night I had a fit of the blues. The game had ended in a draw and once again, I had not reached double figures. Prescott had got another 50 odd and, in the opinion of most, had saved our side from a beating. Conversation was desultory as it had been at dinner.

As usual most of them were listening attentively to Anthony Bathurst. He was well launched on a theme that I had heard him discuss many a time before in his rooms at Oxford. "The Detective in Modern Fiction." It was a favourite topic of his and like everything that aroused his interest, he knew it thoroughly—backwards, forwards, and inside out.

I caught his words as I entered the room.

"Oh—I admit it quite cheerfully—I look forward tremendously to a really good thriller. I'm intrigued utterly by a title like 'The Stain on the Linoleum.' But, there you are, really good detective stories are rare."

"You think so?" interjected Major Hornby, "what about those French Johnnies, Gaboriau and Du Boisgobey?"

"Like the immortal Holmes," replied Anthony, "I have the greatest contempt for Lecoq. Poe's 'Dupin' wasn't so bad, but the majority—"

"You admire Holmes?"

"Yes, Mr. Arkwright, I do! That is to say—the pre-war Holmes!"

"You don't admit that his key is always made to fit his lock?"

"Of course," replied Anthony, "that must be so! But he deduces—he reasons—and thereby constructs. The others, so many of them, depend for success on amazing coincidences and things of that nature."

"You think Holmes stands alone?" queried Mary.

"Not altogether, Miss Considine, as I've often told Bill Cunningham." He turned to me, "Mason's M. Hanaud, Bentley's Trent, Milne's Mr. Gillingham, and to a lesser degree perhaps, Agatha Christie's M. Poirot are all excellent in their way, but oh!—the many dozens that aren't."

"I could mention three others," said Jack Considine.

"Yes? Who are they?"

"Bernard Capes' 'Baron' of *The Skeleton Key*, Chesterton's Father Brown, and H. C. Bailey's Reginald Fortune."

"I am willing to accept two," said Anthony, "but Father Brown—no. He's too entirely 'Chestertonian.' He deduces that the dustman was the murderer because of the shape of the piece that had been cut from the apple-pie. I can't quite get him."

The company laughed merrily.

"Ah, Mr. Bathurst," remarked Sir Charles. "There is a great gulf between fiction and real life. Give me Scotland Yard every time."

"I am ready to. Scotland Yard is a remarkably efficient organization—but—"

"Well, Sir Charles, I think this! Give me a fair start with Scotland Yard, and its resources to call upon, if necessary, and I'll wager on my results."

"What about that trumpeter?" from Gerry Prescott.

"Never mind that. I was asked for my opinion and I gave it."

"In the event of your being on the spot at a murder case, then, you consider that you would solve the mystery quicker than trained men?"

"Under equal conditions, yes, Captain Arkwright! Again, what is a trained man? I am a trained man. I've trained myself to observe and to remember."

Here, Lady Considine interrupted with "Pardon me, Mr. Bathurst. But these girls won't sleep if you keep on discussing murders. Besides, Sir Charles wants his game of Auction."

Two tables started, the military party playing solo. And gradually the hum of conversation subsided as the games got under way. Helen Arkwright played while her sister sang. Jack Considine and Anthony went into the garden to smoke cigars. I stayed and watched the cards. Prescott won steadily from most of them, but from Lieutenant Barker chiefly. And when after a time, I saw a look of more than ordinary chagrin pass over the latter's face and following that, an I.O.U. handed across the table to Prescott, I felt that they had played long enough. For neither

Sir Charles nor Lady Considine cared for such happenings as that. So at eleven-forty or thereabouts, I suggested they stop.

The others assented readily.

"I'm for bed," I said, "after just one 'spot'!"

I walked to the French windows that commanded the garden and looked out. The rain that had come on just before seven, had ceased and there was a moon with a sparkling retinue of stars.

I swallowed my whisky.

"Good-night, you fellows."

"Good-night, Bill!"

At the foot of the staircase just in the shadow of the heavy banisters, I passed Prescott and Barker, deep in conversation. The conversation stopped as I approached.

"Coming to bed?" I interrogated.

"Not yet," replied Prescott. "Time's young yet. Besides I have—"

I didn't wait for his sentence to be finished.

Our bedrooms were on the second floor—seven of them in a row along a long corridor that ran the length of the house. All the men were together. Jack was in the biggest—the first—that night he was sharing with Anthony—then came in order, Daventry and Robertson together in No. 2, Hornby, Prescott, Tennant, myself, and Barker last. On the first floor was the billiard room, directly facing the stairs as you ascended, and the bedrooms of the other members of the family.

Each one of the bedrooms on the second floor was fitted with a bathroom and shower. There was a connecting door in each room, leading to the bath. This connecting door in each instance faced the door of the bedroom opening out on to the corridor. It was a fancy of Sir Charles Considine, this, and much appreciated by all those privileged to enjoy the hospitality of Considine Manor. I shall never forget that night.

I slept but little, a most unusual state of affairs for me.

I was strangely uneasy, and it was not till close on five o'clock that I fell into a doze.

And if I never forget that night, I shall never forget the memory that followed it!

For I was awakened by a piercing scream that echoed and re-echoed through the house. It came from the floor below!

"Murder! Murder! Help! Help! Murder!"

## CHAPTER II
# IN THE BILLIARD ROOM

IT WAS a woman screaming! Not that I'm in the position of having frequently heard men scream. But the feminine note in the voice was apparent to the most careless listener.

I hastily threw on a blazer, pulled on a pair of slippers, opened my bedroom door, and came out into the corridor.

Everybody's door seemed to open simultaneously.

Leaning over the banisters, it was easy to tell that the screams were coming from the billiard room.

We dashed down the staircase, the crowd of us—white-faced and anxious—as men and women are, when suddenly aroused by shock! And as we came to the billiard room door, I was conscious that we were one short—and something told me whom we lacked. I was soon to know for sure.

For as I entered the room that held the horror that had brought us flying from our beds I could hear Sir Charles Considine's voice rising authoritatively above the hum of excitement, "Gentlemen, gentlemen—please—whatever the trouble is—one of you stay outside and keep the ladies from entering."

Across the bottom of the table face downwards, the right arm hanging limply over the side, lay Gerry Prescott. He lay partly on his right shoulder, and it was easy to see how he had met his death. A dagger had been driven fast into the base of his neck, at the top of the spinal cord.

The shock hit us all hard, and the chatter of the girls, querulous and interrogative, although just outside the door, seemed vaguely distant.

Marshall, the maid, who had given the alarm, stood shaking against the wall, her affrighted eyes staring at the body of poor Prescott.

"Get back to your room, Marshall," said Sir Charles. "I'll see you again later." His ordinary pomposity of manner seemed to have deserted him.

"What can we do, sir?" said Arkwright.

"He's past all earthly help," muttered Anthony.—"Been dead, I should say, some hours."

"Terrible, terrible, in my house too," went on the old man. "I shall never. . . ."

"May I suggest, sir, that perhaps Jack and Arkwright should get a doctor and the police here, as quickly as possible?" said Bathurst.

"Yes, yes, my boys, excellent!"

"And of course we must touch nothing. Look!" He pointed round the room. Then went and whispered in Sir Charles's ear.

"Certainly, Bathurst. Capital suggestion. You and Jack get along, Arkwright. And all the rest of you go, please, to the garden except Mr. Bathurst and Bill Cunningham. No good can be done by crowding round."

Hornby, Barker, Daventry and the others did as they were bid, very pleased I think to get into the wholesome fresh air! And I turned to look at what Anthony had pointed out.

Three chairs were overturned on the floor, the other side of the table, and by the side of one lay the poker from the billiard room fireplace.

The window at the further end of the room, overlooking the gravel drive that ran along that side of the house was open at the bottom—at least, a couple of feet. Prescott was fully dressed. As far as I could judge in the same clothes as he had worn the previous evening. Dinner jacket, wing collar, bow tie, dress shirt, to my eye exactly as he had dined. An exclamation from Anthony arrested my attention.

"What's he wearing brown shoes for? Eh"—rubbing his hands—"Bill, I fancy I've got my chance after all. Do you see that, Sir Charles? Brown shoes! And what is more"—he crowed with excitement—"one hasn't got a lace."

"My God!" said Sir Charles, "you're right. Perhaps he dressed in a hurry."

Anthony was shaking his head. "Perhaps," he muttered, "but—" Sir Charles turned to us, agitation on his face.

"It has just occurred to me," he said, "you don't think anybody in the house . . .?"

Anthony shook his head again. "It's a bad business, and I can't tell you anything till the police come. There are several questions I require answered."

This time it was my turn to provide the sensation.

"Sir Charles," I cried, "look at the dagger! Don't you recognize it?" He adjusted his pince-nez, and went across to the body.

"Good God, Bill! It's the Venetian dagger off the curio table."

"What's that?" Anthony's eyes gleamed with excitement. "Your property?"

"Been in the family two hundred years. An ancestor of mine brought it from Italy."

"Where was it kept?"

"On a table in the drawing-room!"

"I don't like it," murmured Anthony. "Why was it brought up here?"

"I have it," cried Sir Charles. "It's burglars after all. Poor Prescott heard them and. . . ."

"It's no good theorizing, Sir Charles . . . without facts to go on! When the police come and deal with points that I can't possibly touch yet . . . I may be able to help you."

No sooner had he finished speaking than Jack's voice was heard outside. "This way, doctor . . . in here."

Dr. Elliott entered. Jack followed him. Close on their heels came Arkwright with an Inspector of Police, and a man who was apparently his assistant—in plain clothes.

"This is Inspector Baddeley, of the Sussex Constabulary," said Arkwright. "I was lucky enough to find him at the station." The Inspector assented.

"Good-morning, Sir Charles. Good-morning, gentlemen."

12 | BRIAN FLYNN

"This is a bad business, Sir Charles," declared Dr. Elliott. "It hardly seems credible that only yesterday this poor fellow. . . ." He went to the body.

The Inspector followed him.

"Quite dead, gentlemen—hum—hum—been dead several hours."

The Inspector carefully withdrew the dagger.

"Try that for any prints, Roper," he muttered. "It's just on the cards."

"Yes, sir," replied plain clothes; he at once got to work with the "insufflator."

"Then photograph the body from both sides of the room."

Roper retired; to return in a few minutes with a camera.

"I think it would be better for you, Baddeley," declared the doctor, "if you had a good look round before I make my examination. I can do nothing and the cause of death is pretty obvious. The murderer knew his business, too! A blow at that part of the spinal column—effective—and to all intents and purposes instantaneous."

"Very well, Doctor. These gentlemen—Sir Charles?" he queried.

"My son, my son-in-law, Captain Arkwright, Mr. Bathurst and Mr. Cunningham, guests and very old friends."

"I understand. All staying here, I presume?"

I took a look at him, carefully. Anthony, I observed, was following my example.

We saw a man of soldierly bearing, dark hair, closely cut to the head, a small moustache neatly trimmed, two steady blue eyes, and an alert and thoroughly business-like manner that completed a make-up which I was convinced belonged to one who would make no mean opponent for the cleverest criminal.

"Is the body exactly as found?"

"Exactly," replied Sir Charles.

"Who found him?"

"The housemaid. Marshall, by name."

"Time?"

"About half-past seven, I should say. You will see her?"

"Shortly."

"Room as it was?"

"Entirely. Nothing has been touched. We were most careful," said Sir Charles. "Mr. Bathurst here," he smiled, "was most insistent on that point."

"Really! Very good of him."

He turned and flung a quick glance in Anthony's direction.

"Thank you," smiled back Anthony. "I'm rather interested in this sort of situation."

"Yes. A lot of people are till they find one. Roper, get those photographs and I'll get to work."

Roper, with camera, did his work quickly and quietly. Baddeley went through Prescott's pockets.

"Absolutely empty, gentlemen. He's fully dressed, too."

"Not quite, Inspector," said Anthony. "Look at his shoes!"

"Good Lord! Fully, but not properly, eh? Tut—tut—extraordinary." His eyes brightened. "And a lace missing—why, oh why, oh why?" And then authoritatively—

"Sir Charles, none of your guests must leave this morning, till I have seen any of them I consider it necessary to."

"As you wish, Inspector. Tell them all, Jack."

Jack Considine slipped out.

"Got all you want, Roper?" Baddeley strode across to the window.

"Not been touched—eh?" He bent forward—eager—attentive; then leaned out across the window sill. Then I think he sniffed and rubbed his hands together.

"We're progressing, Mr. Bathurst. Don't you think so?"

Anthony joined him and I could see he was puzzled.

"You can get on now, Dr. Elliott," declared Baddeley. "I want to have a look outside. Come along, Roper." They went out.

Sir Charles heaved a sigh of relief.

"Most distressing!" he said. "When he was looking at me I felt like a murderer myself. I think we'll leave Dr. Elliott to his job for a few minutes and go and dress decently."

Anthony lingered for a moment or two, then followed us out.

Within a short time he joined me in my bedroom. Like me, he had taken the opportunity to shave and dress.

"Sit on the bed, Holmes," I said, "the tobacco is not in the Persian slipper, but the cigarettes are on the dressing-table."

He took one.

"Bill," he said, "I'm worried. This is a beastly business."

"No clues?" I said.

"On the contrary, too many! I can see too much light. It's part of me to distrust the too-glaringly obvious."

"Dashed if I follow you. Tell me of these clues that have hit you so forcibly."

"Listen then. We have the following indisputable facts:

"(1) Prescott is found dead in the billiard room—stabbed with a weapon with which you all appear to be familiar.

"(2) There is evidence of a struggle.

"(3) The window of the room is wide open—distinctly suggesting the entrance of an outsider—or possibly the exit.

"(4) This is most important—he is fully dressed with the exception of the shoes—one of which is minus a lace. And there is mud on those shoes.

"(5) His pockets are empty—pointing to robbery.

"(6) He was murdered between twelve o'clock and five o'clock—approximately. We shall learn more from the doctor as to that." He paused. "All very significant. And I have three other clues at the moment which exercise me considerably. Two in what I will term 'Group A' and one in 'Group B.' That is to say—they don't exactly fit." He blew a smoke-ring and shook his head.

"What are they?" I queried excitedly.

He grinned. "I'm holding 'em for the time being, old son. Don't be in such a hurry. All good Watsons have patience as their longest suit."

"I can't see any motive," I complained.

"Find that, Bill, and you'll be two-thirds of the way to the solution. In a few minutes I'm going to have a good look round. I'm going with Baddeley when he comes back from the garden."

"Where to?" I asked. "Where will he go then?"

"Well, if he's got any sense—and I'm confident he has—to Prescott's bedroom."

I nodded my head wisely.

"To see any—"

Sir Charles's voice outside, broke in upon us without ceremony.

"Dr. Elliott wants us all in the billiard room," he called. "All those of us who were there before."

We accompanied him downstairs.

Dr. Elliott seemed to be bursting with importance.

"Tell Inspector Baddeley at once—please," he cried. "Sir Charles, will you please arrange for Baddeley—"

"I have already done so, Doctor," rejoined our host.

We waited, expectant. What had the doctor to tell us that we didn't know?

Baddeley entered—Roper following.

"Well, Doctor, what's the excitement? There's something very interesting outside. The more I see of this case—the more it—"

"Sir Charles—Inspector—I have carefully examined the body of this poor young fellow"—he paused dramatically—it was *his* moment—"and I find that he died not from a stab as we all presumed and supposed, but from asphyxiation!

"Gentlemen, he was strangled by something tied tightly round his throat! Look at the peculiar colour of his face—look at his tongue!"

## Chapter III

## MR. BATHURST AND THE BED-CLOTHES

"What!" snapped Baddeley. "Strangled? Strangled with what?"

"I can't say exactly," replied the doctor. "Look at this mark"— he pointed decisively—"it runs right round his throat. The thing has been tightened at the back of the neck. String! Tape! Anything that would bear the strain. Look at the mark on the flesh." We looked. The impressions were certainly vivid. They had been hidden from us, partly by reason of the dress collar, and partly by the position of the body.

"But where is the tape?" muttered Baddeley.

"Rather, Inspector," cut in Anthony, "ask your question in a slightly different form."

"What do you mean?"

"Say—Where is the shoe-lace?"

"By Moses—but you're on the spot, Mr. Bathurst." He turned with the utmost excitement. "That's why the lace is missing! I must see everybody, Sir Charles, I really must."

Anthony leaned over and looked up the dead man's sleeves, with a curious, quizzical expression.

Baddeley regarded him playfully.

"I've no doubt somebody in the house has got something up his sleeve, Mr. Bathurst, but I don't think it can be this poor fellow." Anthony smiled back.

"He has a handkerchief—Inspector!"

The Inspector then delivered a question that was surprising. I confess it startled me.

"Can any of you tell me reasonably accurately, what time it started raining here last evening?"

"I can," I answered. "The rain started about ten minutes to seven."

"And ceased—when?" he followed up.

"It was not raining," I said, "at a quarter to twelve."

"How do you know? Were you out?"

"No, Inspector," I replied. "I happened to look out into the garden about that time and the stars were shining—that's all."

"H'm! Sure of your time?"

"Quite."

"Now, gentlemen," Baddeley turned to us all with a gesture that contained a certain amount of defiance and, at the same time, the fleeting hint of an apology—and he seemed to gain from it an added sense of dignity—"I need your help. And because I need it—I'm going to ask for it."

"Ask on," said Anthony. "I'm your man."

"Well, I feel like this, Sir Charles and gentlemen, this isn't an ordinary case. Can *any* of you; you, Sir Charles, Mr. Bathurst, Mr. Cunningham—or you, gentlemen"—he turned towards Arkwright and Jack—"tell me of anything you know that puts any motive into this affair? Any incident that throws any light on it whatsoever?"

We shook our heads.

"Frankly, Inspector,"—Anthony spoke for us—"we are as much in the dark regarding the whole affair as you yourself are."

Baddeley went on.

"Very well, gentlemen. Then we know where we are. But I may as well tell you that Mr. Prescott was in the garden last night—after 12 o'clock—and he was not alone! But I'll find out who was with him! And what's more, I'll find the scoundrel that murdered him!" He squared his shoulders.

"You're certain of what you just told us?" queried Anthony.

"I am."

"How are you certain?"

"That's my business, Mr. Bathurst. Try your hand at finding things out yourself."

"Right-o!" Anthony accepted the challenge laughingly. "Shall we go fifty-fifty with our discoveries?"

"If it suits me." He turned to Sir Charles.

"I should like now, Sir Charles, to see Mr. Prescott's bedroom."

"Certainly, Inspector."

"May we accompany you, Inspector?" suggested Anthony.

"You may—if you keep moderately quiet."

We ascended the stairs.

Sir Charles leading the way, stopped outside Prescott's door. "Perhaps, Arkwright," he said, "you and Jack would get back to the others. They must be having a pretty thin time. Tell them to have any breakfast they care to, and that Inspector Baddeley wishes to interview them all before he goes."

Baddeley called Roper on one side. He seemed to say something quickly and imperatively, and I fancied I heard the words—"and keep your eye on her all the time."

"A new development—hear that?" I whispered to Anthony.

He came last, preoccupied.

"Nine stairs, Bill! Nine stairs. Nine stairs—Inspector."

Baddeley looked puzzled. Then walked to the bedroom door.

"Of course," he said, "anybody could have been in here since, couldn't they? The door is shut. But not locked. The key is on the inside. But I can't tell for certain that these facts were so when Prescott left it for the last time, can I?"

"I think you may take it so," said Sir Charles somewhat pompously. "My people here wouldn't think of entering another's room."

"Somebody here thinks of murder, Sir Charles, say what you like! What about the servants?"

"They have not been on this floor yet."

"Very good."

We made our way into the room.

As far as I could see there was nothing to excite the slightest comment. Between us and the bed, upon our immediate right and left was the dressing-table and a chair respectively.

With its head to the left-hand wall, as we entered, stood the bed—that is to say, almost in the far left-hand corner of the room. A door opposite to us opened on to the bathroom that I have previously described. In the far right-hand corner stood a large Sheraton wardrobe.

"Well, he went to bed last night, did Mr. Prescott," said Baddeley. "That's pretty clear at any rate. And he got up in a hurry!"

The bed certainly showed signs of recent occupation. All the normal and ordinary signs of a person having slept there were clearly and distinctly indicated, the bed-clothes being in disarray and lying trailingly on the floor between the bed and the door of our entrance.

The Inspector was quickly at work.

He crossed to the dressing-table and examined it carefully. He then came back to the bed, lifted the pillows, and peered inquisitively beneath.

"Strange—" I heard him mutter. I turned to Anthony who was standing with his eyes fixed intently on the bed. He seemed to be following an acute train of thought.

"Sir Charles," broke in Baddeley. "There's one thing that every man has to a degree, and yet this young fellow Prescott appears to have been entirely without—unless he'd been systematically robbed."

Sir Charles lifted his eyebrows. "Yes?" he queried.

"Money—cash—whatever you call it. How do you account for this? He has no money in his pockets, he has no note-case in his pockets. His pockets are all beautifully empty. I say to myself he dressed in a hurry—I shall find his money in his bedroom. Either on the dressing-table or under his pillow. People have different places of putting their cash you know, gentlemen. But I don't find it! And it puzzles me!"

"It's certainly very strange, Inspector," said Anthony. "But there may be the possibility that his small change had run out, and that he has put a note-case into another jacket. Let's try the wardrobe."

Baddeley did so. Two more coats hung there. His deft fingers quickly ran over them. "Nothing there," he declared.

Anthony thought again. "Try the drawers of the dressing-table."

Baddeley opened the right-hand drawer. Ties, collars, a handkerchief or two. He tried the left. "Ah!"

He held a wallet—leather—the kind of wallet that is in popular use. He opened it.

"Stamps—and private papers—no money—not a note there—I'll run through these papers later," he said. "But not a cent."

"Is it robbery, Inspector?" questioned Sir Charles. "Appearances, at least, seem to me to be pointing in that direction."

Baddeley shook his head. "Up to now, sir," he declared—"it's got me beat! I find out one thing and seem to see a little light, and then I chance on something else, equally important on the face of it, that knocks my first theory into a cocked hat. Nothing fits! Nothing tallies!"

"I confess that to some extent, I share your bewilderment, Inspector," said Anthony. "If I knew—"

Baddeley suddenly became vividly alive. "Of course—there may be that explanation." He swung round on to the three of us. "Any cards last night?"

"Yes," I replied. "Why?"

"Never mind"—impatiently—"Prescott playing?"

"Yes."

Anthony became all interest. "I see your drift, Inspector."

Baddeley grinned. "Qualifying for a mental hospital—I've been—haven't I?

"Now, Mr. Cunningham," he turned to me—"you say you saw Prescott playing—I'll tell you something more—you saw him lose and lose, now didn't you? He was cleaned out of all he had, wasn't he?" he brought his fist down on the dressing-table triumphantly—"*he lost the lot?*"

Anthony's eyes held me inquiringly.

"Yes, Bill?" he murmured. "What about it?"

For a brief moment I felt majestic. I had a curious sense of power. "This is *my* grand minute," I whispered to myself.

Taking a cigarette from my case, I tapped it on the lid with a becoming delicacy.

"On the contrary, Baddeley," I weighed my words with a meticulous distinctness. "On the contrary—Prescott won! Systematically, consistently, and heavily."

Baddeley stared as though unable to believe the words. Anthony let out a low whistle.

"Frightfully sorry to upset your pet theories," I continued airily—"but I know that for an absolute certainty."

"How?" snapped Baddeley. "Were you playing with him?"

"No," I replied. "I was watching."

"And onlookers see most of the game, Inspector," said Anthony.

"Who was playing?" insisted Baddeley.

"Almost everybody—except Mr. Bathurst, Mr. Jack Considine and myself."

He scratched his chin, reflectively.

Then came the question that I was half-expecting.

"Anybody in particular lose more than most?"

I hesitated before replying, and I sensed that he detected the hesitation.

I crossed the Rubicon! "I think Lieutenant Barker was the heaviest loser, but he would, doubtless, let you have that information. Surely, you don't imagine—"

"That's all right, Bill," said Anthony. "The Inspector can easily satisfy himself."

I made a mental note to tell Anthony as soon as the coast was reasonably clear of the Barker I. O. U. That had certainly not come to light.

"Any idea who was the last person to be with Prescott, last night?" asked Baddeley.

I reflected. After all, it was best to be candid with this man.

"I can't answer that for certain," I said, "but I can tell you this. I went to bed about a quarter to twelve, and on my way I saw Prescott in conversation with Lieutenant Barker."

"Where?"

"At the foot of the staircase."

"Anything in the nature of a quarrel?"

"No," I answered with rapid decision, "the conversation as far as I could gather was just ordinary conversation. Naturally, I didn't listen to what they were talking about."

"H'm, I suppose not."

Baddeley sat on the chair and put his head in his hands. "As soon as I've looked round," he observed, "I shall have to interview everybody."

Anthony strolled across the room, round to the left-hand side of the bed.

"Not much room here, Inspector," he said. "Hardly enough space for a fellow to dress—eh?"

Baddeley looked up from his reflections, distinctly unimpressed.

"He would find plenty of room to dress the other side, Mr. Bathurst—there's every indication of it." He indicated the appointments.

"You think so," replied Anthony. "So do I. And unless I receive an unexpected set-back I really believe things are moving."

I was frankly amazed. I turned over all that I had heard, all that I had seen and as I pondered over them, I couldn't for the life of me see how the slightest light could possibly have come to him.

"I presume, Inspector, you will see the people within a little while, eh?" he inquired.

"That is my intention, Mr. Bathurst. Why do you ask?"

"Well, I'm going to have a little tour outside, if it's all the same to you, and Bill Cunningham's coming with me. Let's hear from you when you're ready and waiting. Come along, Bill."

He walked out, down the stairs, through the hall and into the garden.

Anthony took out his pipe and filled it.

"Before I do anything more, Bill," he said slowly, "I'm going to sit on this seat and smoke this good tobacco—and you can do likewise."

"Good!" I uttered. "Tell me what you think."

"No"—shaking his head—"I can't do that, just yet. For Baddeley will be well on with his work of cross-questioning before very long, and there are some things I wouldn't tell my mother—just yet."

"Please yourself," I grunted. "But what puzzles me," I said, "is the *scene* of the crime as the journalists say. What took Prescott to the billiard room?"

"There are three reasonable solutions to that," puffing at his pipe, "one—an assignation, two—he was called, drawn, or attracted there by something he saw, heard—or perhaps was afraid of happening—and three—he was taken there."

"By force?" I interrupted.

"Perhaps. There were, if you remember, *certain* signs of a struggle."

"The fact that he was fully dressed," I countered, "suggests to me very strongly that there was an assignation."

"Yes, I concede that, Bill, but against that, you know, I must recall to you the brown shoes he was wearing."

"Perhaps his dress shoes weren't handy," I argued. "The others may have been nearer to his hand."

"No. I can't have it, Bill, his dress shoes were under his chair by the bed—just where he put them when he took them off last night. You see, I looked for them."

"Oh," I said, rather nettled. "You evidently thought them important."

"Most assuredly," he rejoined. "But not so important as the other thing Prescott's bedroom told us." He rose and stretched his arms.

"Yes," I assented. "That money business of Baddeley's is very mystifying. And yet there may be a perfectly simple explanation."

"Of course," said Anthony. "But I wasn't thinking of that."

"What do you mean?" I broke in. "What else was there?"

"My dear Bill," came the reply, "I want you to come with me now and have a look at the ground immediately below the billiard room window."

"Yes, but—that bedroom—what else did you—?"

"What else did I notice? Let me see, now. What was it? Oh—I found much food for thought, my dear Bill, in the somewhat peculiar disposition of the bed-clothes."

## Chapter IV

# UNDER THE BILLIARD ROOM WINDOW

"Peculiar?" I queried wonderingly. "Nothing about them struck me as peculiar. Anybody getting up in a hurry would have thrown them off just as they appeared to—"

"You think so—well, you may if you like—here we are."

We had progressed along the gravel drive until we were opposite the billiard room window. This lay on our right. Separating the path where we were from the window in question, there was a bed of roses approximately ten to twelve yards in width.

"What Baddeley has found, Bill, we can find," muttered Anthony. "There you are—look. Footprints—that interested Baddeley."

His face shone with eagerness and intensity.

"Keep on the path, Bill; leave these to me."

He stepped carefully on to the earth bed, examining the prints with the utmost care. From where I stood I could see a number of well-defined "treads" and I readily appreciated the importance attached to them by both Baddeley and my companion. It was very evident that one person at least had crossed the rose-bed pretty recently to get beneath the billiard room window. It looked an outside job of course. Burglary evidently—Prescott had heard noises—come down to investigate—found the trouble in the billiard room and had interrupted the disturbers at the cost of his own life. But would burglars strangle their assailant with a shoe-lace? Surely not! The whole affair seemed to me to be most intricate and most involved. Still, the rain of the evening before had been a Godsend—there were the footmarks—telling some story to more than one pair of eyes. They might help the Inspector and I knew they would interest Anthony.

I looked across at him. He was evidently at a loss. Something on the wall beneath the window of the billiard room had apparently excited his attention. He scrutinized it most carefully, and then turned again to the prints. He shook his head.

"Bill!"

"Hullo?"

"Come over here, will you?"

I complied.

"Now, Bill, look at what I am going to show you, very carefully. I expected to find traces of Prescott somewhere out here—you, of course, noticed the mud on the shoes he is wearing—so that Baddeley's announcement came as no surprise to me. The natural place to look for them was in the vicinity of the billiard room window, since that room was the last room he can have entered. Now, look here! Do you see that double line of tracks? Looks something like a 10, I should say. We can bank on those being Prescott's. I'll make sure later—but I'm certain of my ground."

"In a double sense," I grinned.

"Eh? Oh—I see—" he laughed. "I wasn't thinking of what I had said. But do look. Here we have a distinct set of tracks that are undoubtedly Prescott's, side by side with a similar set, undoubtedly again Prescott's, leading in the reverse direction. The left-hand set, as we face the window, lead to the path, and the right-hand set lead to the window. Agree?"

I looked attentively at the footmarks. "Yes. It would seem so."

"Right," he rejoined. "Then—proceeding along that line of argument—since Prescott eventually reached the billiard room and stayed there, the tracks leading to the path should have been made first. That's elementary, isn't it?"

Once again I assented.

"Now," continued Anthony, "cast your weather-eye over there."

He pointed to a few feet away from the tracks we had agreed were Prescott's.

I stared and started in surprise.

"More!" I cried.

"True, O King," said Anthony, rubbing his hands with real showman instinct, "and whose are they? Come and look closer." They belonged to a much smaller foot.

"A woman?" I queried.

Anthony shook his head in disagreement. "I think not. Might be. But it's broad for a woman, not suggestive of a woman's heel, and more generally indicative of a medium-sized man. He has walked deliberately towards the window from the path and then equally deliberately back again. That's another point I'm basing my opinion on, a woman so often picks her way, especially with any mud about. Put it down to feminine fastidiousness."

"Then Prescott did have an assignation?" I ventured.

"Perhaps! It certainly looks like it. But—"

"But what?"

"Well, there's nothing to prove that the two people that have been here were here at the same time, is there? Of course, I'm willing to admit that in circumstances of this kind, the balance of probability is that they *were*. But one never knows. I wonder what Baddeley—"

"What do you *really* think about it?" I urged.

His answer amazed me rather.

"Too much!"

"What do you mean?"

"Exactly what I say. I *am* actually thinking too much about a *number* of points. There are too many clues here, Bill, falling over one another. No wonder Baddeley's mystified. My job is to separate the true significances from the false. That's real detective talent, Bill. In this case, there is so much that *conflicts*. One set of facts, for example, points to the North, and another set, apparently just as authentic, points unerringly to the South. Therefore, they can't, all of them, be authentic! See? Some must be false. And I've got to pick 'em out." He slapped me on the back. "Magna est veritas"—he stopped abruptly.

"Now what?"

"By Jove!" he murmured. And an illuminating smile spread across his features. "Of course. Of course."

He turned to me quickly.

"It's strange, Bill, how an occasion will turn up to illustrate the exact truth that a man has just enunciated. Here's an example to hand. I was talking about the separation of falsehood from truth. Effecting this separation explains something very clearly that has been causing me no end of bother."

I became all attention and interest, immediately.

"Explain," I said. "Put me out of my miserable ignorance."

"Look at this wall, then."

I looked. "Yes, what about it?"

"Well, Bill, it's like this—listen! Assuming Prescott was out here some time last night or this morning, how would you suggest he got here? Did he come downstairs and risk the possible disturbance of other people or did he come from his bedroom down the nine stairs to the billiard room and out via the billiard room window? Think before you answer."

I hesitated a moment.

"Well, of course, it's all guesswork—"

"Not for a moment, old son! Use the powers the good God has given you."

I nodded sagely, yet still uncomprehending; then burned my boats.

"Down the stairs and out of the window!"

"You think so? Let's investigate. I suppose that window, Bill, is roughly fifteen feet from the ground—eh?"

I assented. "An easy job," I interjected, "for an active man!"

"And when he wanted to get back," replied Anthony, "a moderately easy climb. He could use the water-pipe," he indicated with his hand the water-pipe running down the wall on the right of the window—"for a hold with his right hand, could dig his toes in the brickwork; clutch the window-sill with his left hand and easily draw his body up. Agree, Bill?"

"Absolutely," I concurred. "If you like, I'll try it here and now, to prove it's a practicable possibility."

"Done with you, Bill. You're a stout fellow! Up you go!"

I suited the action to the words. Reaching out with my right hand I gripped the water-pipe well up its length, pulled myself up a bit, kicked at the brickwork with my toes, got a momentary hold, hung for a second, shot up my left hand to clutch the window-sill, succeeded, and hauled myself up. Entrance to the billiard room would have been a comparatively simple matter.

"Satisfied?" I grinned. Then, dropped to the ground again.

"Completely! So that, friend Bill, is the method by which the now defunct Prescott, poor fellow, got out and got back? Eh?"

"That's about the size of it," I agreed, feeling a sense of triumph. "We've established that pretty firmly."

Then I woke up.

"I disagree!" said Anthony curtly.

"You disagree?" I muttered in amazement.

"I do! And I'll show you why. I warned you to get that grey matter of yours to work—didn't I? Pay attention to what I am going to demonstrate."

"Go ahead!"

"I'm going. Now, Bill, which would be the easier way to get out of the room? To get out, using the reverse method by which you got up—that is to say—leaning out for a grip of the water-pipe with one hand, and then all the rest of the movements, or as you said, a simple drop from the window-sill?"

"A simple drop, unquestionably," I answered, without any hesitation.

"I think so, too! Where then," he swung round on me, alive with interest, "are the heavy marks of his feet when he dropped? The ground is soft, remember. And he was a pretty hefty fellow. There's no sign of a drop at all—only this double line of tracks. Look!"

It was as he showed. There were no indications whatever of anybody having dropped from the window.

I stared at him, for the moment nonplussed. Then turning, caught his eye. I could see that there was more to come.

It came! "Also, Bill, I would call your attention to two very important facts. Important, that is, in relation to the line of investigation that we are at present conducting. Look at the toes of your shoes."

I did as directed.

"Slightly scraped," I said ruefully, "getting up to that window of yours."

"Exactly, laddie. Exactly. Now for important fact number two."

"I'm all attention."

"Well, just as the wall has had its effect on your shoes, so have your shoes had their effect on the wall. See?"

He pointed to the brickwork. It was quite true. My shoes had made a perceptible discoloration where they had rubbed as I had struggled for my foot-grip.

"And what is more, Bill," continued Anthony, "it's compara-tively dry now. Last night was wet, remember. And it may interest you to know that the wall was perfectly clean when I arrived here just now, and Prescott's shoes are certainly not scraped."

"Sure?" I queried.

"I am. I'm carrying a mental photograph of Prescott about with me, and you can take it from me, Bill, that Prescott never did the climbing trick that you've done this morning. Now where are we?"

"Ask me another," I grunted. "I should think, more in the dark than ever."

But Anthony dissented.

"I'm not so sure of that. I'm beginning to see a little more light."

I surveyed him with astonishment.

"What on earth—"

"I'm still holding on, Bill, so don't worry me. Come along here, we'll do a little more prospecting."

We strolled back along the path that led back to the French doors.

"No indication here of which way either of them went," remarked Anthony. "This gravel path hardly takes a foot's impression, which, at the best, would be hours old by now."

He stopped by the French doors. "Yes, Bill, I'm in the dark still with regard to many points. As I said to you previously, there are so many things that don't fit, they seem extraneous to the real core of the crime—all the same, at the risk of becoming monotonous, I think I can see a glimmer of light."

"What's your next move?" I questioned.

"I want to have another look around Prescott's bedroom. I should also like to glance at his papers—but Baddeley pouched those—his check-book might be interesting too. Yes, I must have another look up there."

"How are you going to manage it?"

"This way. I'm going to ask Sir Charles to cover me by engaging me, so to speak, to clear up the affair on his behalf. You know what I mean. Terrible disgrace to Considine Manor, and all that, to have this mystery unsolved. Poor young fellow done to death, in a charming English country house, where he is staying as a guest. Must get to the bottom of it for the sake of the family name, you know. Otherwise, if Scout Baddeley finds me poking about too much in bedrooms and around footprints, he'll take the bull by the horns and arrest A. L. Bathurst, Esq. Get me, Bill?"

Truth to tell, it did seem pretty terrible to think that a delightful place like Considine Manor could harbour the crime it did. It was another English summer morning after the rain of the night before. It seemed to breathe freshness, and grass, and new-mown hay, and butterflies and cricket—all that pageant of hot July that no other country in the world can give.

"What about Canterbury?" I ejaculated.

"Giving it a miss! I can't very well rush off and bury myself in a round of gaiety after what's happened here. Besides, I shouldn't be surprised if Baddeley has something chatty and snappy to say about any of us leaving yet awhile at any rate."

"Have you let them know?"

"No, I'll wire later. Let's get back now, and I'll see Sir Charles."

We strolled back, and the reflection came to me how suddenly our immediate outlooks had changed. A few hours ago Anthony had the prospect of a glorious week at Canterbury. Similarly, I had been anticipating a delightful time in various delightful places—an English country house takes a bit of beating during real summer—and now! Look at it how you would—this sinister affair inevitably impinged in some way on the lives of all of us who were staying in the house. I, for one, try as I might, could not shake off its shadow.

Sir Charles met us as we entered the house, a changed man from the morning before.

"I wanted a word with you two men. I'm perfectly assured that you will understand—it's nothing really to do with me, or anything—er—over which I appear to be able to exercise any control—but Inspector Baddeley has intimated to me—I must say, that, for a policeman, he put the matter very, very tactfully—I might even go so far as to say—delicately—that he wishes to interview all of us in the house, as soon as possible. I suggested we resort to the library."

"That's all right, sir," responded Anthony. "Is he waiting now?"

Sir Charles looked at his watch. "I have made arrangements for the proceedings to—er—commence in half an hour's time."

"Could I have half a word with you, sir?" asked Anthony.

"Delighted, Bathurst."

"I've always been attracted by affairs of this nature, sir, little thinking that one day I should be swept into one. Would you be good enough to give me *carte blanche* as it were, to do a little investigating off my own bat? With your authority, you see, acting in a private capacity as your agent, I can satisfy Inspector Baddeley of my bona fides if he catches me nosing into things." Sir Charles pondered for a moment, and I fancied his reply came after some degree of hesitation.

"I see no objection, Bathurst. Provided, of course, that any—er—results of your inquiry—are submitted to me before any action is taken."

"I'll promise you that, sir—readily!"

"Very well."

"Then we'll regard that as settled."

"This will entail your staying on here," continued our host. "I've discussed the question with nearly all the others, and I've put it to them, subject to the Inspector's permission being granted that they leave as quietly as possible to suit their several conveniences. After the interview, of course. No good purpose whatever can be served by any of them staying, and no lack of respect will be shown by them to the dead, if they leave in the manner that I have described. If any one of them should be required for the inquest—I am sorely afraid that an inquest is unavoidable—Inspector Baddeley will be furnished with full particulars. This will enable the authorities to get into touch quickly, should it be necessary."

"What about Prescott's people, sir?" I ventured.

"He has no father, Bill, and is the only child of his mother. Jack is communicating with her, I believe, almost at once. Somewhere in Blackheath, I fancy. I dread the task of meeting her. Still more I dread the task of telling her." He blew his nose fiercely to cover his evident agitation.

The other members of the party came thronging up. But a hush seemed to have descended upon them. The conviviality of last night and the excitement of the morning's awakening had departed. They had heard, indistinctly yet definitely, the flutter of the wings of the Angel of Death. He had passed them by, but he had been very close to them. And now what awaited them? Grief to the young is a transient matter. It soon becomes impossible—youth's ardent eagerness engulfs it. It must be so. Grief can find no permanent habitation in the heart of youth. Lady Considine thought of Mrs. Prescott, and the news that would so soon reach her. One mother considered the anguish of another mother. Mary seemed terribly shaken, most of the men looked unperturbed; no matter what their feelings were, they were clever enough to mask them.

The servants did most of their work on a kind of mental tiptoe. We waited. But not for long.

A quick step and a quick voice sounded upon our ears.

"I am at your service, ladies and gentlemen," said Inspector Baddeley.

## CHAPTER V
## THE METHODS OF INSPECTOR BADDELEY

"I DON'T suppose this is going to be a very pleasant job for the ladies, Sir Charles, and you can rest assured that as far as lies in my power, I'll make it as smooth and easy as possible. So I propose, with your approval, to talk to you gentlemen first. I should prefer to see my clients separately, and, as was your suggestion, I think the library will serve the purpose very nicely."

He turned to Roper.

"You come with me, Roper. I may want you."

Sir Charles Considine coughed—then, very quietly but nevertheless very determinedly—interposed. "That seems to me a trifle one-sided as a proposition, Inspector. You have support, physical, moral, and also no doubt intellectual," he smiled somewhat whimsically at Roper—"and we, all of us, are, to an extent, shaken by the terrible event that has befallen my house, and, therefore, as a consequence are neither so self-controlled nor so mentally alert as normally. We appear before you to be questioned and cross-examined. I don't think I should be asking an unwarranted favour if I suggested that you allow, say, two members of my circle to be present while you conduct your examination. H'm? What do you say, Inspector?"

Baddeley met his gaze for a moment, as though making an attempt to fathom his real intentions. Then with a laugh and a shrug of his eminently business-like shoulders, gestured his consent.

"Choose your men. On the condition that I see the three of you first."

"Thank you, Inspector. Believe me, I appreciate your courtesy. I should like Mr. Cunningham and Mr. Bathurst to—er—um—*assist* you in your intended investigations."

"As you wish, sir, and thank you. Now, with your permission, you three gentlemen will do me the goodness to accompany me to the library, and we will do our united best to see if we can't, by hook or by crook, throw some light on this unfortunate affair. And you, Roper! I've been lucky enough to unravel some pretty ticklish problems in my time, some by good luck, some, if I may say so, gentlemen, with pardonable pride, by intelligent application to the matter in hand. And I hope," he turned on us all decisively, "to hunt the truth out, *here.*"

We entered the library. Our host motioned us to our seats. Baddeley took the armchair at the head of the table investing himself as far as he could with an atmosphere of the inquisitorial. Roper took the chair on his left. Sir Charles placed himself in front of the fireplace, while Anthony and I took chairs at the side of the table.

The Inspector was soon in his stride.

"Now, Sir Charles, this Mr. Prescott, whose death we all deplore, was a guest of yours?"

"Yes. For my cricket week."

"Known him long?"

"No. It would help you materially, if I informed you of the circumstances of the acquaintanceship. Prescott was at Oxford with my son and Mr. Cunningham here, and we met him at Lords' during the last 'Varsity Match—just a month ago. We invited him here for our annual week."

The Inspector was impressed. "Is he G. O. L. Prescott then—that played for Oxford against Cambridge?"

"He is, Inspector! And there's one more fact that I had omitted to mention, he had met my daughter, Mary, some months previously."

"Where?" Baddeley's face betrayed keen interest.

"At Twickenham, in December."

"You have no reason to suspect, Sir Charles, that any developments had transpired from these meetings?"

"None whatever. As far as my knowledge goes, Mr. Prescott and my daughter entertained no feelings for each other, beyond those of mere friendship."

"I see." Baddeley fingered his chin. "You've seen nothing during his stay here, that you consider might have any bearing upon his death? Nothing—however seemingly unimportant? Think, Sir Charles!"

The old man shook his head. "No, Inspector. I've noticed nothing at all unusual, nothing that could possibly touch his death. The scene this morning came as a terrible shock to me. And as terrible by reason of its utter unexpectedness as by reason of its horror."

"How much money did Prescott lose last night, Sir Charles?"

"Really, I've no idea! But nothing worth worrying about—you can set your mind easy on that point. I shouldn't allow it—in Considine Manor."

The Inspector raised his eyebrows.

"Then, in light of your answer, you may be surprised to know that there was some pretty high playing at Considine Manor last night."

The eyes of our host flashed with his reply. "Very surprised and exceedingly annoyed. Had I known, had I had the slightest inkling—you are certain of what you are stating—pardon me?"

"I make that statement, Sir Charles, on unimpeachable authority."

"Dear, dear! This news disturbs me profoundly."

The old man's appearance confirmed the truth of this last statement. This unexpected revelation, following upon the shock of the murder, had made its mark upon his countenance. He huddled himself into a chair. Then braced himself to ask another question.

"Was Prescott playing high?"

"He was, Sir Charles." Baddeley's features relaxed for a fleeting moment into a smile—"and incidentally, he won a considerable sum of money."

"Whom from?"

"That you shall hear, sir, during the course of this morning's inquiry."

Sir Charles subsided again, by no means so sure of himself as he had been. I could not help whispering to Anthony as he lounged in his chair with his long legs extended—"First blood to the Inspector."

He grinned, and as he did so Baddeley's next question came.

"Now you, Mr. Bathurst. A guest here, also?"

"Yes."

"Like Mr. Prescott?"

"Didn't know him sufficiently to express an opinion."

Baddeley evinced his annoyance. "I didn't mean did you like him, Mr. Bathurst, what I meant to say was, were you a guest of Sir Charles under similar circumstances?"

"Sorry! I misunderstood you. No—not exactly. My invitation is only a day or two old."

"Did you know the murdered man?"

"No, I did not. That is to say at all well. I've run against him at Oxford."

"Did you see anything while you were here, or did you hear anything during the night that you think worthy of mentioning to me?"

"Nothing at all, Inspector."

"You were not playing cards, last evening?"

"No, after dinner when the cards started I strolled into the garden with Mr. Jack Considine. We were there about twenty minutes. Then we went to bed—and like everybody else were awakened by the maid's discovery in the billiard room. Which she celebrated in the usual manner."

"H'm—any theory in regard to the crime, Mr. Bathurst?"

"Yes, Inspector."

"Based on?"

"What I've seen this morning."

"Let's hear it."

"You shall. All in good time. After all—it's merely a theory."

Baddeley was obviously disconcerted by the reply. I don't think he knew quite what to make of Anthony.

So he turned his battery on to me.

"Mr. Cunningham? Sir Charles tells me you're an old friend of the family."

I bowed. "Of many years' standing. And a regular guest for the Considine Cricket Week as you may guess."

"Know Prescott?"

"Moderately. Played cricket with him at Oxford—not much beyond that."

"Know anything about his private affairs?"

"Nothing."

"And last night, Mr. Cunningham. What can you tell us about that?"

"I was in the drawing-room after dinner with the others, and as I have previously told you, I was a watcher of the card-playing party. I went up to bed about a quarter to twelve."

"Where was Prescott then?"

"I left him in conversation with Lieutenant Barker."

"And of course you heard nothing during the night?"

"I'm afraid not."

"Bill," interjected Anthony. "Tell me this. When Jack and I went into the garden for a smoke, was everybody in the drawing-room? Think carefully."

I considered for a moment—then replied with decision—"Yes—everybody."

"You didn't see anybody leave it?" he reiterated.

"To the best of my belief," I asserted, "everybody save you and Jack was in the drawing-room."

"Right."

Baddeley pushed across a letter.

"Have a good look at that, Mr. Cunningham."

"Yes?" I queried.

"That's a letter addressed to Mr. Prescott. I think you may know the handwriting?"

I took the letter. It seemed an ordinary enough letter, touching upon the fact that Prescott was shortly visiting Considine Manor, but the portion where the signature would have normally appeared, had been torn off.

"Sorry, Inspector," I replied, "I don't. I can't help you."

I handed it back to him. His glance searched my features for a brief space then—

"Try Mr. Bathurst; does he find the writing familiar?"

Anthony smiled and held out his hand. He read the writing with interest and turned the letter over with apparent curiosity.

"Where did you find this, Inspector?"

"Sorry, Mr. Bathurst, but you mustn't expect me to give away all my secrets. Tricks in every trade, you know." He laughed lightly. "As you were good enough to remark just now—all in good time. Let's come to the point, the handwriting—recognize it?"

"I've never seen it before, so I can't. But I think, before the case is over, that I shall probably see it again."

Baddeley flung him a challenging glance. But Anthony's eyes met his and never for an instant wavered. Then they both smiled.

"Try Sir Charles Considine," countered Anthony. "He might know it, though I don't fancy so."

Sir Charles straightened himself in his chair. He extended his hand. "Let me look, Baddeley, though why Mr. Bathurst is so confident that—no, no," shaking his head in dissent, "to the best of my knowledge and belief, this writing is new and therefore strange to me. What's the date—my eyes aren't as good as they were?"

"July 22nd," responded Anthony, with the utmost readiness, from the other side of the table.

I fancied that the Inspector threw him an approving glance, but I remembered his uncanny memory for dates, and their associations. He had seen the letter and had mastered its detail—that was all. Baddeley gave the letter to Roper. "Keep that handy," he muttered, "we haven't exhausted all the possibilities." Then to Sir Charles: "I should like to see Mr. Considine junior next, Mr. Jack Considine, is it?"

Our host bowed—"As you wish."

"Just tell him, Roper, will you?" from Baddeley quietly.

"And as most of us have had very hasty breakfasts, gentlemen, I'll get Fitch to bring us a little light refreshment," chimed in Sir Charles. "We seem destined to be here some little time." He rang the bell, as Roper entered with Jack Considine. Fitch followed them.

Sir Charles delivered his instructions, which were promptly carried out.

"Mr. Considine," said the Inspector, "sorry to trouble you—but—can you throw any light on this business?"

He proceeded to question him on similar lines to those he had just employed with us.

Jack told him all he knew, and I was just beginning to think that it was all a business of ploughing the sands when I was startled out of my convictions.

I had vaguely heard the question repeated for the fourth time—"did you hear anything during the night?" and was just as vaguely prepared for the denial when Jack Considine gave an answer that made us all sit up and take notice.

"Well, Inspector," he said, a little diffidently perhaps, "now I come to think over things very carefully, I have rather a hazy recollection that I heard something that I may describe as unusual."

"What was it?"

"I am pretty certain that I was half awakened during the night by the sound of a door shutting. It might have been something different, but I don't think so. No," he continued reflectively, "the more I try to reproduce in my ears the sound that I heard, the more convinced I am that it *was* a door shutting."

"Ah!" rejoined Baddeley. "Near you? Or distant?"

"That's awkward to answer. As I stated, my awakening was only partial, it is difficult to measure sound when one is half asleep . . . but I should say pretty near."

"Any idea of the time?"

"None! I didn't trouble. I wondered at it in a sleepy sort of way . . . and went to sleep again."

Baddeley pondered for a moment.

"I understand, Mr. Bathurst, that you have been sharing Mr. Considine's bedroom. Did you hear anything of this?"

"No," came the reply. "I heard nothing—I was tired and slept very soundly, as is usual with me."

The Inspector nodded.

"We may take it then," he proceeded, emphasizing his points by a succession of curious little fingertaps on the table, "that Mr. Considine heard this door shutting more because of his half-awake condition than through any particular—er—nearness or proximity to the place where it occurred—eh? You grasp my point?"—turning to Sir Charles.

"You mean," interposed Anthony, "that had this door shut very near to our bedroom, the chances are that I should have heard it, too?"

"Exactly," answered Baddeley. "Don't you agree with me?"

Anthony meditated for a moment. "Perhaps. It's certainly possible—but on the other hand—perhaps not. I might and I mightn't."

Our interrogator then came back to Considine.

"Did you hear anything after you heard this door shut, Mr. Considine?"

"No! I simply turned over and went to sleep again."

"Think very carefully, sir. Pardon my insistence, but very often things come to us out of our sleeping moments if we only concentrate sufficiently." His eyes fixed Jack, and held him and once again I caught a glance of the man's efficiency. There was no brilliance there, no subtlety beyond ordinary astuteness, no flashing intuition bringing in its wake an inspired moment, but merely a species of machine-like efficiency. I have repeated the word, I am aware, but I can think of no other, at the moment, that so adequately expresses the quality that I perceived. I contrasted him with Anthony Bathurst. One the product of "the Force," hard-bitten in the school of personal industry, bringing a well-ordered brain to bear on the problem that confronted us, the other, public school and 'Varsity all over, with a brilliant intellect nursed by the terminology of these institutions, treating the affair as an adventure after his own heart. What would Baddeley have done, I found myself wondering, with the other's opportunities? Where would Anthony have cleared a passage, had he been born Baddeley? My musings were short-lived.

"Let me have that letter again, Roper?" demanded the Inspector. And once again was the letter produced and inspected. And once again was the writing unrecognized; it conveyed no more to Considine than it had done to us.

Then Anthony surprised me. "Do you mind if I take another glance at it?" he asked. "Something has just come to my mind."

Baddeley looked at him shrewdly and curiously for a moment.

"Certainly," he agreed, and passed the letter over.

But one look proved satisfactory.

"I'm sorry—I'm wrong," muttered Anthony, "I can't help you."

The Inspector smiled at his apparent discomfiture. He seemed agreeably relieved to discover that A. L. Bathurst was human after all; and followed on to the next stage of his investigation.

"I think that will do for the time being then, Mr. Considine," he said. "And ask if I can see—in order, if you please"—he referred to some notes that he took from the pocket of his lounge jacket, "first Mr. Robertson, then Mr. Daventry, and then Mr. Tennant?"

Robertson entered. He hadn't bargained for this when he accepted the invitation to Considine Manor.

He could tell the Inspector nothing, except what he knew concerning the cards. He could not identify the writing of the letter.

He had known Prescott at Oxford—just casually—that was all. He had slept soundly, only to be awakened by Marshall's scream, as we had all been.

Daventry and Tennant, in turn followed him, only to be similarly ignorant and similarly dismissed.

Baddeley sipped a glass of port and munched a biscuit. Sir Charles followed suit approvingly.

"Well, what now, Inspector?" he remarked. "We appear to have reached an *impasse*. What is your opinion now?"

"Plenty of time yet, sir," came the reply. "I've by no means exhausted my possibilities of information yet." He referred again to his list, then looked up—"There are three gentlemen to be seen yet, Major Hornby, Captain Arkwright and Lieutenant Barker, then there are three ladies, and finally some of the servants. I'm sorry, Sir Charles,"—he swung round in his chair and confronted him—"but somebody in this house knows something about last night's job—and I'm stopping on till I lay my hands on him—or her. So ask Lieutenant Barker to step this way."

# Chapter VI

# LIEUTENANT BARKER ATTEMPTS TO REMEMBER

I GLANCED in Anthony's direction. Evidently the Inspector imagined that Barker knew something, or perhaps as an alternative he fancied that he in his turn knew something about Barker. I scanned Anthony's face in the idea of ascertaining, if I could, if he attached any degree of importance to the man we were awaiting. Personally, I couldn't see Barker as a murderer . . . he was a chap whom I had always liked, no end of a decent sort . . . surely they didn't regard him in that light . . . it seemed to me ridiculous . . . preposterous. . . .

"Come in, Barker," said Sir Charles Considine kindly. He, too, seemed to sense the hostility in the atmosphere and appeared to be desirous of putting the man at his ease, were such a thing possible. "Inspector Baddeley, as you are fully aware, is conducting a little inquiry into the terrible tragedy that has—er—overwhelmed us this morning, and would like to feel that any information you can give him in the matter, you will do so unhesitatingly. Understand, m'boy?"

Barker smiled. He had one of those sunny smiles that run, so to speak, in all directions across the smiler's face. You know what I mean—the eyes light up, and the whole face seems radiantly happy. This was a blue-eyed smile, and I always think that's the finest variety.

"Delighted, sir," he answered. "May I sit down?"

He seated himself in the chair that Baddeley proffered him. The latter leaned across the table in his direction.

"I am relying on you, Lieutenant Barker, to be perfectly frank with me," he said.

"Fire away, Inspector," smiled the Lieutenant.

"How many tables were playing cards last night?"

"I really couldn't tell you, Inspector. I believe Sir Charles Considine here was playing 'Auction' with some of the others—Sir Charles can confirm this if you ask him, and give you full particulars—I really didn't pay much attention—but I was playing 'Solo' myself with Major Hornby, Robertson and Prescott. You've seen Robertson already, hasn't he told you?" His teeth flashed into another disarming smile.

"And you lost money, didn't you? Consistently?"

"That seems to me my business, Inspector, but I'll be perfectly open and frank . . . I did."

"Remember, Lieutenant Barker," snapped Baddeley, "we are investigating a murder, and a singularly brutal murder at that, not the theft of two pennyworth of tripe."

"I do, Inspector," responded Barker with an almost affected languidity, "that was the sole reason I answered you. Rest assured that I certainly shouldn't have done, otherwise."

Baddeley glared. Then his experience gained the victory over his temper.

"Do you object to telling me the amount you lost to the dead man?"

Barker hesitated momentarily. Looked up at the ceiling and tapped his foot on the carpet. Then, to all appearances, came to a decision.

"I'll tell you. I suppose it's your job to nose into things. I lost over two hundred pounds—two hundred and eight, to be strictly accurate."

"Did you pay it over there and then?"

Barker flushed under his tan.

"I gave Prescott an I.O.U. for the amount," he said very quietly.

I felt rather than saw Anthony straighten himself in his chair. And I was relieved to think that Barker, having furnished the information regarding the I.O.U. himself, I should be saved the unpleasant business of telling Anthony as I had intended. Baddeley's voice cut into my thoughts. It rang with expectancy.

"Now then, Lieutenant, you gave that I.O.U. to Prescott?"

"Yes."

"What did he do with it? Do you know? Can you remember?"

I am certain that Barker hesitated ever so slightly over his reply, and I caught myself wondering if one of those machines they use in France for measuring heart-beats or something—or the time a suspected person takes to answer pregnant questions—would have registered and recorded this almost imperceptible hesitation. The answer came, however, and perhaps not quite what I anticipated.

"Yes! He put it into his pocket wallet."

"Certain?"

"I watched him—it meant two hundred and eight pounds to me, did that tiny piece of paper."

"Tiny? How tiny?"

"Half an ordinary-sized envelope. I tore an envelope in half to write it."

"By Moses! this is important, Lieutenant Barker. Do you realize the importance of it?"

"Possibly I do."

"I've been through Prescott's papers—I've been through that wallet arrangement you spoke about—that I.O.U. has vanished!"

But Barker met his almost accusing eyes—unflinchingly.

"How can you be positive as to that?" he urged. "Prescott may have put it anywhere, since placing it in the wallet—it might conceivably be in a dozen places!"

"There is no trace of that I.O.U. in Mr. Prescott's bedroom—nor among his belongings. I've looked for it. And I can't find it. I may as well tell you that it had a special interest for me, because I deduced its existence, there's no harm that I can see in telling you how. I knew Prescott had won money, several witnesses can prove that—and I knew also that it was a good-sized sum. It was distinctly unlikely that cash would pass for a large amount. Therefore I suspected an I.O.U."

"I might have settled by check for all you know," muttered Barker.

"Possible, but the chances are—*no!*" replied Baddeley. "Gentlemen don't usually carry their check-books in their dress clothes." This laconically.

"Prescott had no money anywhere, had he, Inspector?" asked Sir Charles.

"Not a coin, sir—he was robbed as well as murdered. But this is a significant fact, he was only robbed of cash. Not of anything else."

"May I ask Lieutenant Barker a question?" from Anthony.

Barker raised his eyebrows.

"When you gave Prescott your I.O.U. was it at the card-table or after you rose?"

"At the card-table—directly we had finished playing." The answer came promptly and abruptly.

"So that," and here Anthony spoke with extreme deliberation, "at least two people saw it passed over? Eh?"

"Hornby and Robertson undoubtedly," continued Barker. "There may have been others near."

"Can you recall anybody?"

Barker reflected. "Captain Arkwright and his wife were standing close by—Mrs. Arkwright had just come from the piano—and I rather think her sister was with them—I can't remember anybody else."

I interposed.

"I saw you give the I.O.U. to Prescott—I was standing by the French doors."

Baddeley flashed an angry look at me.

"You didn't tell me that, Mr. Cunningham," he remonstrated.

I "finessed." "I told you Prescott won money," I argued. "I couldn't think of everything on the spur of the moment."

Anthony intervened.

"That's all right, Bill. The Inspector understands that."

Baddeley, however, had not finished with Lieutenant Barker.

"When you had handed your I.O.U. over, what did you do?"

Again I imagined that I detected a certain hesitation in his answer.

"I chatted for a few minutes with Prescott over the amazing luck he had . . . then I went upstairs to bed."

"Prescott go with you?"

"N-no! He gave me the impression he had something he wished to do."

"That's so," I interjected again, "I spoke to him as I went up, and I gathered something similar."

"Then you went straight to bed?"

"Yes!"

"Didn't speak to anybody after you got upstairs to your bedroom?"

"No—yes, I did," correcting himself. "I sang out 'good-night' to Hornby, Robertson and Cunningham here. If you call that speaking to people."

"The three of them? Where were they?"

"Not exactly *to* them, Inspector, but as I passed their bedroom doors. I walked down the corridor and called out 'good-night' to them as I went. See?"

"Why to those three?"

"Because I knew they were there. They were the only three whom I had seen go up. Bathurst and Jack Considine were in the garden."

Baddeley nodded in acquiescence, and accepted the explanation.

"Did the three people answer you?" suddenly queried Anthony.

"Lord, what a memory I'm expected to have," groaned Barker. "Let me think." He passed his fingers through his hair. "I can only recall that Major Hornby answered, with any certainty. But that may perhaps be because I know his voice best. I can't answer for the others."

"What do you say, Bill?" continued Anthony.

For the life of me I wondered what he could see in a point of detail like this. I hesitated.

"Did you hear him, Bill? Did you answer him? Is his memory correct? These little things count so much in a case of this kind. What do you say?"

I thought very carefully. Had I any accurate remembrance of what Barker said he had done? Yes! I had!

"Yes," I replied. "I heard Lieutenant Barker go by along the corridor, and I answered him. Perhaps he failed to hear me."

"Good," muttered Anthony. "You were occupying the last bedroom along the corridor, weren't you, Barker, and you, Bill, the last but one?"

We nodded in agreement.

Then Baddeley cut in. "Hand the Lieutenant that letter we found in Mr. Prescott's bedroom, Roper," he ordered.

Lieutenant Barker took it.

"Know that handwriting?"

"Never seen it! Absolutely certain on the point." He handed it back.

Baddeley appeared almost to have expected this answer. Perhaps he was getting used to it by now. He drummed on the table with his finger-tips.

"Anything more, Inspector?" asked Barker.

"For the time being, no thank you," was the answer, when Anthony, who had been leaning across the table chatting to Sir Charles, broke in.

"I'm awfully sorry to trouble you, Barker, but I'd be eternally obliged . . . was last night the first night that Prescott had won much?"

Barker shifted uneasily. "From me. . . . Yes!"

"That isn't quite what I asked you," continued Anthony relentlessly.

"By Moses," cried the Inspector, "this case fairly beats the band for a lot of tight-lips."

Barker looked from one to the other. Then he suddenly seemed to realize the value to himself of the information that was his to give.

"The night before last," he answered a trifle obstinately, perhaps sullenly is the happier word, "he won a considerable amount from a brother officer of mine."

"Major Hornby?"

Lieutenant Barker bowed.

Anthony turned to the Inspector. "Inspector," he said, "gentlemen are traditionally 'tight-lipped' when it comes to what they regard as 'telling tales.' I think you have misjudged Lieutenant Barker."

Barker blushed, he was the type of Englishman that finds praise embarrassing. But Baddeley did not take his semi-rebuke passively.

"Gentlemen do lots of funny things," he declared. "Even to fracturing the Sixth Commandment."

"Now, I've a second question . . ." proceeded Anthony.

"You stated a few moments ago that your I.O.U. to Prescott was half an ordinary-sized envelope. You said you tore an envelope in half to write it. I am not quite clear as to your exact meaning. Do you mean that your I.O.U. was half an envelope or half the *back* or *front* of an envelope? You get my meaning? There's a difference if you think it over carefully."

"I see what you mean, Bathurst. I slit an envelope down the side with my finger, separated the back from the front, then tore the back in two and used a half."

"I follow you! So that your I.O.U. would have measured say two inches by three?"

"Just about."

"Thank you! That's all I wanted to know."

Barker bowed to Sir Charles and retired.

"You seem to be able to extract all the information you require, Mr. Bathurst," said Baddeley. "Much more successful than I am."

Anthony grinned. "Put it down to my irresistible charm of manner."

His tone altered. "Who's next? Major Hornby?"

The Inspector nodded in agreement. Sir Charles Considine rose. "I'll convey your message." He passed through the door.

"We are now going to have a few words with Lieutenant Barker's 'brother officer,'" declared Baddeley, "and military blood is thicker than . . . ."

Sir Charles entered with the Major on his heels.

Baddeley commenced with a direct action. In this instance the attack came early.

"Of course, Major," he said, "doubtless you are quite cognizant of the fact that you are not bound to answer any of my questions . . . all the same, I hope that you will . . . your rank and position have taught you that Duty is very often unpleasant . . . but nevertheless remains Duty . . . it is my Duty as an Inspector of Police to prosecute these inquiries . . . however much against the grain. . . ."

Major Hornby's face remained set . . . immovable.

"Your apologies are unnecessary, Inspector," he said.

"Apologies? You misunderstand me . . ." Baddeley was floundering now, a trifle out of his depth . . . these people were different from those of his usual encounters . . . he went straight to his objective . . . safer, no doubt.

"We have been informed, Major," he remarked, "that on the evening before last, you lost a large sum of money to Mr. Prescott."

"Quite true."

"How much?"

"The amount doesn't concern you, Mr. Inspector, that I can see."

The muscles of Baddeley's face tightened. But despite the rebuff he stuck manfully to his guns.

"Did you pay him or . . ."

"Don't be insultin' . . ." Baddeley winced as though he had been stung.

"You refuse to answer my question?" he retorted.

"On the contrary—I have answered it. I told you not to be insultin'!"

The atmosphere had become electrical. Two or three times Sir Charles had half-risen from his seat in a deploring kind of manner—a venerable peacemaker. Anthony watched with keenest interest while Roper remained inscrutable, the perfect subordinate.

"I don't appreciate your attitude, Major Hornby," insisted the Inspector, "and perhaps it may not be extended to the consideration of this letter"; he held his hand out to Roper, who passed the letter across to his chief once again.

"Do you know that handwriting?" he asked in a curt voice.

Major Hornby flung the letter on the library table contemptuously. "I do not! It's not addressed to me, and therefore has nothing whatever to do with me. Also, I'll wish you a very good-morning." He left us!

"Tut, tut," commented Sir Charles. "This is very unfortunate!"

Anthony smiled. Then burst into laughter.

"Sorry I don't possess your irresistible charm of manner, Mr. Bathurst, nor yet your keen sense of humour," put in Baddeley.

"If all people were like that specimen that has just departed, Justice wouldn't often be appeased and many murderers would survive to exult over their crimes. I'm not sure, however, that he hasn't proved of some assistance. In murder, motive must always be pursued first. To whose benefit was the death of this man Prescott? A burglar? Or somebody inside the house? Which? When I can answer correctly to those two questions, I shall be nearer a solution. For both have possibilities." He paused. Then turned to Sir Charles again.

"I hope Captain Arkwright will prove more reasonable."

Sir Charles replied.

"My son-in-law will help you all he can . . . for my sake."

Now Dick Arkwright was a white man. One of the best, all the way through, and I felt assured that whatever his father-in-law's wishes were he would fall into line. His marriage with Helen Considine had been a love-match and it was patent to all observers that it had brought no regrets with it. His consideration for his wife carried with it consideration for the members of her family, particularly for the head thereof.

"Captain Arkwright," said Baddeley, "I have very little to ask you, and as a consequence, I will not detain you for more than a few moments. That is of course assuming that you have nothing to tell us?" He paused.

"I am sorry to think that I am unable to help you, Inspector, by supplying any facts of importance, beyond those with which you are already acquainted," Arkwright said.

"I appreciate that. Thank you. First, take a look at that letter. Know the handwriting? No? Thanks! Secondly, your bedroom, Captain Arkwright, is the nearest to the door of the billiard room—it is on the same floor—with Sir Charles'—did you hear any noise in the night, any sounds of the struggle that appears to have taken place there?"

"No, Inspector! I can't honestly say that I did. But I have a very hazy recollection that I heard footsteps in the garden not so very long after I had gone to bed. I can't be sure even of that—and yet the sound of footsteps seems to belong to my last night's sleep! Have you ever experienced anything of the kind, gentlemen?" he appealed to all of us,—"and I have a reason for telling you. As a matter of fact," he continued, "the reminiscence was so vague, so entirely nebulous, that I had decided to say nothing about it. But something has happened to make me change my mind."

"What is that?" demanded Baddeley.

"Mrs. Arkwright heard them too," he replied quietly. "But she can't place the time."

Baddeley nodded his head in apparent confirmation. "I'm not surprised." There was a respectful tap on the door.

"Come in," called Sir Charles. Fitch, the butler, entered. He went to our host. "Wants me at once, Fitch?" muttered Sir Charles.

"If you please, Sir Charles."

"Excuse me for a few moments, gentlemen. Lady Considine wants me immediately." Fitch held the door open. We waited. But not for long. Sir Charles was quickly back, agitated, breathless, but alert.

"Inspector Baddeley," he said, "I have news for you at last. Lady Considine has been robbed of her pearls—the Considine pearls."

## CHAPTER VII
## LADY CONSIDINE COMPLICATES MATTERS

"I OUGHT to tell you gentlemen, or at least those of you to whom the Considine pearls are unknown, that they have been in my family for several generations and are of great value. My wife wears them in the form of a necklace that she had made some seventeen years ago. And it has been her fancy, call it whim if you please to, to wear this necklace quite often. The last occasion she wore it was the evening before last—it was my birthday and it delighted her to celebrate the affair. She informs me that she replaced the necklace in her jewel-case when she retired that evening. I ought to mention that it goes into a case of its own which, in turn, is placed in a larger case. Unfortunately, she did not take the trouble to get this second case at the time—she was very tired. Yesterday morning she asked Coombes, her maid, to do so for her. About half an hour ago, it occurred to her that Prescott's death may have resulted from a clash with burglars. She went to her large jewel-case, and was amazed to discover that the case containing the pearl necklace was not there. Neither was it to be found—anywhere. She is terribly upset to think that her partial neglect may have cost this poor young man his life."

Baddeley waved his hand deprecatingly.

"There is no need for Lady Considine to worry over that, Sir Charles. None of us ever know the result of some of our most innocent actions. But this requires careful consideration. Coombes—this maid of Lady Considine's—is she to be trusted?"

"As far as I can say," replied Sir Charles. "She has been with us seven or eight years. She is desperately worried, Lady Considine says, and has no definite remembrance as to whether she replaced the necklace or not. Will you see her?"

"I will see both Lady Considine and her maid in a few moments. But I should like to feel certain whether I am investigating one case or two."

"Things certainly are moving, Inspector," said Anthony. "But perhaps this latest piece of news will help us a lot."

Lady Considine was heart-broken at her loss. But she did her best to forget her personal loss in the greater sorrow that had befallen others. She was a pretty woman, and I knew that she had been considered a beauty in her day.

"When I went to bed the night before last," she said, "I took the necklace off and put it into its own case, but I did not put this case into the larger one. I was sleepy and it meant getting up and crossing the room. My maid was brushing my hair. I said, 'Coombes—put the case with the necklace away, in the morning—never mind now. Hurry up with my hair and I'll get to bed.'"

Sir Charles interrupted here.

"I understood you asked her the following morning."

"No, I asked her that night. To put the case away in the morning."

"Did she reply?" commented Baddeley.

"She promised that she would."

"Did you remind her again the following morning?" he continued.

"Yes—first thing."

"And then what transpired?"

"Nothing. I thought no more about it. Not seeing the case lying on my dressing-table, I naturally imagined that Coombes had carried out my instructions."

Baddeley nodded in acquiescence. "Quite so. And then?"

"Well, I was thinking over this dreadful business of last night and worrying . . . and wondering . . . when suddenly the idea of theft and burglary flew to my brain . . . and as I have just explained to Sir Charles . . . I went straight to the large jewel-case, unlocked it . . . more as a means of making sure than because I really thought I had lost anything . . . you know the rest. The case containing the necklace was not there."

"Now, Lady Considine," said the Inspector, "try and think . . . when is your last remembrance of seeing the missing case?"

"Yesterday morning."

"You are sure . . . quite sure?"

"I am." Then turning to her husband, "I want Inspector Baddeley to see Coombes—poor girl—she's in a terrible way. I think she can already visualize herself being hanged at least. But as honest as the day, Inspector, so don't frighten her."

"I'll try not to, I'm sure," grunted Baddeley. "Roper!"

The silent Roper came to life again.

"Get full particulars of this missing necklace from Sir Charles and take the usual steps. If you send for Coombes," to Lady Considine, "I'll see her now."

"Enter Coombes L.U.E.," smiled Anthony. "As innocent as the 'rathe' primrose by the river's brim."

"Don't count chickens before the hatching stage is completed, Mr. Bathurst. I've known crooks that looked like choristers, and bishops that looked like burglars."

"That comes of judging people by their looks, Inspector," chaffed back Anthony, "instead of by their actions."

Coombes entered. Scared to death! She was a tall girl, with wispy red hair and a big face. The sense of bigness was given by the face, by a long line of strong jaw. It was what I should have called a "horse's face." Pythagoras would have declared that she had transmigrated from a horse. She opened the proceedings by bursting into loud sobbing.

"It's all my fault, Mr. Policeman," she managed to get out between her sobs. "I'll tell the truth. I promised mother when I came into service I'd tell the truth *always*, so I'll tell it now, even though I shall cop out for it—but it's all my fault and God's own mercy that we haven't *all* been murdered." She paused for breath.

"Come, come, my girl, what is all your fault?" demanded Baddeley.

"Why, sir . . . this. . . . I d-d-don't believe I put the n-n-necklace case away at all!"

"You mean you left it lying where Lady Considine had left it?"

"Y-y-yes! I meant to put it away first thing that morning when my Lady told me to—but something put it out of my mind and made me forget it . . . and I never saw it again to make me remember it. At least I don't think I did."

"You can't be sure of that, you know . . ." remarked the Inspector. "Because you didn't see it, doesn't prove it wasn't there." He turned to Sir Charles. "Any strange characters been knocking about lately, that you've noticed?"

"None that I've seen."

"H'm! Probably an inside job. With your permission I'll step up to the bedroom in question, a little later on, Sir Charles! Perhaps you gentlemen would care to accompany me? I'll adjourn down here, temporarily. All right, Coombes—you come along with us."

We made our way upstairs—Anthony wrapped in thought.

Lady Considine's bedroom was, as has already been explained, on the same floor as the billiard room. It will be remembered that the door of the latter faced anybody ascending the stairs. Lady Considine's room lay on the left of the landing some twenty yards away. Between her room and the billiard room was the bedroom occupied by Dick and Helen Arkwright.

Baddeley entered, the rest of us following him.

"Is this the dressing-table where the case was?" Lady Considine replied in the affirmative.

"It's near the window. Quite an easy entrance from outside." He walked to the window and measured with his eyes the distance to the ground. "Is the window left open during the day?"

"Quite possibly, Inspector. As you see, it's of the casement type."

He examined it. "No signs of its having been forced," he pronounced.

"I presume the door is open during the day?"

"It's closed, of course, but not locked, if that's what you mean."

"I see! Most people in the house would have a fairly reasonable opportunity of access to the room—eh?"

"I suppose they would," admitted Sir Charles, reluctantly. "This may sound as though we are confoundedly careless, Inspector, but we've always considered ourselves remote from crime. That's the only explanation I can give."

"Surely you don't suspect anyone here . . ." broke in Dick Arkwright. "I'm beginning to think those footsteps I was yammering about were made by real feet. And I feel very relieved to think that I told you."

"I'm not forgetting 'em, Captain Arkwright. Not for a moment," conceded Baddeley. "I've formed some very definite conclusions. Come down again to the library, Sir Charles, and you two gentlemen, also," he addressed Anthony Bathurst and me—"you may as well see the thing through with me." We retraced our steps downstairs to the library.

"Your servants, Sir Charles—tell me about them—I'm curious."

"There's Fitch, the butler, been with me over twenty years, Mrs. Dawson, the cook over fifteen years. The four maids are Coombes, the one you saw—she looks after Lady Considine and my daughter, Mary, if she happens to require her—Marshall,

Hudson and Dennis. I suppose you would call them house-maids. They see to the rooms and wait at table if we want them. Coombes has been with us over seven years, Marshall and Hudson are comparative newcomers to my establishment. Been with me about three years and eighteen months respectively. Dennis we have only had nine weeks. I've no complaints against any one of them."

For a brief space Baddeley conferred with Roper.

I observed that Anthony watched this consultation with some interest.

"Very well, then, Roper—I quite agree," I heard the Inspector say—and then, "ask her to come in." He turned in the direction of Sir Charles. "This maid, Marshall, that discovered Mr. Prescott's body this morning—you say she has been with you for about three years?"

"About that time, Inspector."

"Well, I'm going to have a few words with her. I'm not—"

The door opened to admit Marshall.

She was a dark, rather pretty girl, of medium height—I should have said of Welsh type. When she entered, I was struck by the extreme pallor of her face. The shock of the finding of Prescott's body had evidently affected her considerably. Had I not known that, I should have thought that she was a victim of fear.

"Your name is Marshall?" opened Baddeley.

"Amy Marshall."

"You've been here some time?"

"Three years in October."

"Your daily duties, I presume, took you into the billiard room this morning?"

Marshall shot a scared glance at him through half closed eyes.

"I sweep and clean several rooms before breakfast—the billiard room every morning, as it has usually been in use the night before."

"Was the billiard room the first room you did this morning?"

"No, sir! I had swept and polished two floors before I went into the billiard room."

"Was the door open when you came to it?"

"No, sir, it was shut."

"When you got in the room—what happened?"

"Well, sir, I opened the door with my left hand, I had my broom and things in my right, so that I didn't catch sight of the corpse, sir, till I was well inside the room."

"Then you saw Mr. Prescott? Eh?"

"And that awful knife—" she shuddered as the memory of the scene came home to her again.

"H'm. Was the window open?"

Her black eyes opened wide, intensifying the pallor of her face.

"The window—sir?" she queried. "Let me think." She pondered for a brief moment. "Yes, sir," she declared. "I think so."

"Your pardon, Inspector," intervened Sir Charles, "perhaps I can help you with regard to that point; the window was open, I distinctly remember noticing it." He preened himself.

Baddeley regarded him with a mixture of approval and amusement.

"It was open when I arrived, Sir Charles, but I was later on the scene than you gentlemen.

"Now, Marshall," he continued, "after you saw Mr. Prescott's body—what did you do? Did you go and touch it at all—take hold of the dagger—inquisitive-like—h'm?"

"Touch it!" she gasped. And then again as though she hadn't heard him properly—"*touch* it? Lord love yer"—she relapsed from her acquired manners—"I wouldn't 'ave gorn near it for a thousand quid. Touch it!"

"Well, what did you do?"

"I screamed. And then got up against the wall to support myself—I come over so queer."

"And then?"

"Then all the gentlemen rushed down, and the master told me to clear off."

Baddeley addressed Sir Charles.

"This dagger, Sir Charles, that was used by the murderer . . . I understood, when I was upstairs, that it is your property?"

"It has been in my family for two hundred years. Came originally from Venice and lies on the curio table in the drawing-room. It was in the drawing-room last night."

"So it must have been taken out between last night and the early hours of the morning?"

Sir Charles bowed. "It would seem so—beyond argument."

"Have you finished with me, sir?" interrupted Marshall. "If you 'ave"—her h's were very uncertain and fugitive just now—"I should like to go—I'm feeling far from well. This shock 'as been a great blow to me."

"No—I haven't quite done with you, yet. You have just told me you sweep and clean the rooms."

Marshall nodded.

"What time did you do Lady Considine's bedroom, yesterday?"

Marshall never turned a hair.

"I 'aven't never been in Lady Considine's bedroom since I was engaged. Coombes sees to that as the master will tell you if you ask him! I know my place, and what's better than that—I keep it."

Baddeley looked her straight in the eyes, but Marshall never batted an eyelid.

"What Marshall says is quite true, Inspector," interjected Sir Charles Considine. "Her duties do not take her into Lady Considine's room."

Baddeley accepted the situation with good grace. He tried another tack.

"There were three chairs overturned in the billiard room when you entered it. Didn't that strike you as strange?"

"It did—when I caught sight of 'em. But the corpse caught my eye first—you run across a corpse on a billiard-table first thing in the morning—see whether you notice anything else much—a corpse seems to fill the landscape—you might say. You don't want no 'close-up' of it—believe me."

This was truth and truth with a vengeance, naked and unashamed. There was no mistaking it. Marshall had put the matter in plain unvarnished terms—with all the cheap humour of her class—but her sincerity was undoubted and it struck home. If we had not been concerned in the investigation of a murder, I think most of us would have laughed outright.

Sir Charles Considine shifted in his chair, uneasily and disapprovingly. Anthony alone seemed completely unperturbed.

Baddeley bent across to Roper. I did not catch all he said, but he seemed very importunate with regard to some point or other, and I heard Roper say, "It's all right. . . . I got it when you first put me wise."

"All right then, Marshall," said the Inspector. "You can go now; if I want you again, I'll send for you."

Anthony leaned across the table, his forefinger extended towards the maid.

"One moment, Marshall."

"Yes, sir," she said fretfully.

"You've answered Inspector Baddeley's questions so nicely," he continued, with a smile charming enough to put any member of the gentler sex at her ease—"that I'm going to ask you to answer some of mine." His smile expanded.

Marshall eyed him doubtfully, but seemed to relax a bit.

He scanned her face deliberately—then I saw him hesitate as though puzzled by something. His eyes searched her, seeking. And his glance grew more penetrative in its quality. Something about her was causing him a difficulty. But he threw it off.

"You had done some work this morning, before you went to the billiard room?"

"Yes, sir."

"Would you mind telling me what work?"

"I had swept two rooms, done a bit of general tidying-up and polished the floor of the dining-room."

"Had you polished the dining-room floor just before you went to the billiard room?"

"Yes, sir—just before!"

"What with?" Anthony's voice was tense and eager.

"Ronuk floor polish."

"By Moses!" cried Baddeley, "then it was Ronuk."

Marshall looked the picture of amazement. She had been led to the brink of a morass and even yet failed to realize her imminent danger.

"You wear gloves for polishing floors?" Anthony's tone grew sharper.

"I use a cloth . . . and wear gloves when I'm using it . . ." Marshall replied with a suspicion of sullenness.

"Then why"—cried Anthony,—"when you entered the billiard room and saw Prescott's body on the billiard-table—why did you rush straight to the window, fling it open—and lean out over the window-sill?"

For the space of a few seconds Marshall stared at him in astonishment. Then she swayed slightly and fell into a dead faint on the library floor.

## CHAPTER VIII

## MR. BATHURST HAS A MEMORY FOR FACES

BADDELEY and Roper sprang to her assistance. The rest of us looked at Anthony with bewilderment.

"An elementary piece of reasoning," he said, apologetically. "In fact, upon reflection, Inspector Baddeley takes more honours than I."

Baddeley who was doing his best to bring Marshall round, looked up and waved away the compliment. "I missed my chance," he said.

"You will remember that when our friend here"—Anthony indicated the Inspector—"arrived on the scene, he saw the open window—and immediately had a look at it. I was watching him, and by one of those rare chances of observation, I noticed that something had attracted his sense of smell—he sniffed. And apparently although he detected something—he wasn't quite satisfied as to what it really was. I followed him up—I've a good nasal organ"—he rubbed it humorously—"and I was able to detect round the windows and also round the window-sill, a faint aroma—pungent—faintly spicy. I suddenly deduced furniture polish—you all know the smell. Marshall uses gloves every morning when she wields the cloth with the polish on; you can well imagine how thoroughly impregnated they are with the odour. When she saw Prescott's body—I said to myself—she rushed to this window and opened it—she leaned out—she placed her gloved hands on the sill—why? And then, gentlemen, I was lucky. Adhering to the wooden top of the window frame—the part under which she had placed her finger-tips to push up the window, was a tiny pink fleck of Ronuk floor polish. It had come off the glove. Now—why did she open the window?"

"Is it a crime to open a window?" The interruption came from Marshall herself. She walked unsteadily to a chair. "I've listened to part of what you've said. Are you going to 'ang me for opening a window?"

"You admit you did open it, then?" urged Baddeley. "Why did you lie about it?"

Marshall eyed him fiercely.

"Why did you open it?" he rapped out.

"I forgot about it! What with all your questions and all your cross-questionin' it just slipped my mind. That was why."

"You haven't answered the Inspector's question," remarked Anthony. "Why did you open it?"

"For a breath of air. Seeing that corpse and that dagger fair frightened me it did. I was struck all of a 'eap. Thought I was goin' to faint, I did. My first thought was air—air. So I rushed to the window—then I screamed."

"I see," snapped Baddeley, threateningly. "You were playing to orders—open window first, then scream—eh? Who told you to do that?"

"What d'ye mean?" she exclaimed defiantly. "Who told me! Nobody—I'm tellin' the truth, I am."

"The truth," cried Baddeley incredulously. "You aren't on speaking terms with it. Who told you? Come on out with it. It will go all the worse with you, if you don't."

"I can't tell you no more than what I 'ave," persisted Marshall. "Seeing that corpse on the table was as big a surprise to me as it was to you. And what's more, you 'aven't no right to keep me 'ere."

Baddeley shrugged his shoulders.

"In a few hours' time you'll wish you'd told me the truth, my girl," he said. "Get along now, and don't play any tricks."

Marshall made her exit, sullen and defiant. But she was afraid of something I felt sure.

"May I use your telephone, Sir Charles? Thank you. I'll get on to the Superintendent to send a couple more men up here. Marshall is worth watching."

"Very well, Inspector."

"And I won't trouble to see Mrs. Arkwright or Miss Considine now—or the other servants. I'll make a point of seeing them alone, later . . . will that suit you, Sir Charles? . . . this latest development has made a big difference. Come along, Roper."

They bustled out. Anthony linked his arm in mine. "We'll have a little lunch, Bill, first, and then I'm going to smoke a pipe in the garden . . . there's something hammering at my brain that I can't properly get hold of. . . . I must be suffering from senile decay or something. A little good food and better drink may stimulate me. It sometimes happens."

Lunch over, we adjourned to the garden.

"A deck-chair and a pipe, Bill—I find very useful adjuncts to clear thinking."

"Has that inspiration come to you yet?" I queried.

"No, Bill—but it will, laddie—don't you fret!"

"What's Baddeley going to do?" I asked. "Arrest Marshall?"

"What for—murder?"

"Well, she seems to know something about it—*you* ought to think so, you bowled her over."

"H'm—do you quite know where we are, Bill? Let me run over things for you. Come and sit at the feet of Gamaliel.

"Well, first of all there's the question of motive. Find the motive, say the Big Noises and you'll find the murderer."

"What about Lady Considine's jewels? . . ." I broke in.

"Yes, they do complicate things a bit, don't they? Still, they supply a motive! Prescott may have been murdered by the thief . . . dead men tell no tales. But there are other people with a motive . . . there's Barker," he went on thoughtfully, "possibly Hornby . . . these are the known motives, what about the unknown—eh?"

"The whole thing seems so damned labyrinthine to me," I muttered.

Anthony assented. "Clear as Thames mud, isn't it? But it won't be a bad idea if we sit down and collect our evidence. What do we know as opposed to what we conjecture?" He emphasized the points with his pipe on his finger-tips.

"(a) That when Marshall saw the body—she rushed to the window and opened it.

"(b) That Jack Considine thinks he heard a door shutting during the night.

"(c) That Dick Arkwright (who is supported in this by his wife or says he is), heard footsteps in the garden.

"(d) That Barker's I.O.U. is missing. Baddeley says so!

"(e) That the murder was premeditated."

I started. "How do you know that?" I demanded.

"The lace was removed from Prescott's shoe, my dear Bill. If the murder were one of sudden passion, you wouldn't say 'lend me your shoe while I take out the lace.'"

"Of course," I conceded. "I should have thought."

"Let's get on! Where were we? . . .

"(f) That Prescott appears to have crossed the rose-bed under the billiard room window some time between seven and his death.

"(g) That somebody else did, too—at some time after seven.

"(h) That the Venetian dagger or the poker found on the billiard room floor shows finger-prints."

"What?" I yelled. "How the devil do you deduce that? You haven't examined them! You haven't looked at either of them enough to know that."

He grinned. "William, my lad, you won't always have me to hold your little hand. Didn't you tumble to Baddeley's game with the letter?"

"What letter?"

"The letter he asked us to identify. That was for finger-prints, old son . . . he'd prepared it in the usual way . . . he's got excellent prints of you and me. And of the others." He chuckled. "He had at least two letters he was handing round."

"Why?" I asked.

"He was probably taking three or four people to one letter. Roper was marking them as we fingered them. Roper wrote them while we were in the garden." He chuckled again. "That was how I spotted it."

"How?"

"You remember they were torn, don't you, where the signature should have been . . . well, the first two tears I saw, didn't exactly coincide in shape . . . see . . . that was what I looked at when Baddeley was asking Jack Considine . . . it's deuced hard, Bill, to tear things exactly similarly. Torn, that is, in the way they were torn. He probably used a third letter later on . . . but I wasn't concerned with that."

"Good Lord," I groaned, "and I never knew."

"I'm now proceeding with the last of things *we* know," continued Anthony.

"(i) That Lady Considine has lost her pearls. Anything else? I think not! I think that just about exhausts what we know."

"Prescott was robbed too," I ventured.

"Of how much, Bill?—nobody knows."

I saw his point. Then I broached a matter over which I had felt very curious.

"You told me this morning, after we had been first called to the billiard room that you had three distinct clues—two I think you said, in Group A and one in Group B. What were they?"

"Hasten slowly, William. Hasten slowly. I'll meet you half-way. The clue in Group B was my little triumph that resulted in the discomfiture of Mademoiselle Marshall."

"And the other two?" I persisted eagerly.

"The other two, Bill, are now three. But I haven't developed them properly yet. There's a missing link, somewhere, and until I get it, I'm floundering a bit. What do you make of Marshall?"

"Well," I answered doubtfully—"I think she's afraid of something."

He knocked the ash out of his pipe.

"I'm curious about Marshall—she knows something she hasn't divulged—why did she open that window? Tell me that."

"How about Baddeley's theory?" I put in.

"What? Acting under instructions? Open the window—then scream?" He shook his head. "Don't think so—somehow."

"Do you know, Bill" . . . he went on, "Señorita Marshall's face haunts me rather. I can't get away from it."

"Love at first sight," I chaffed. "All good detectives do it . . . think of Irene Adler."

"No—not that, Bill. Not in that way. It's a different feeling altogether. I can't forget it . . . because I can't place it. . . . I seem to have seen it before somehow. The question is *where?*"

"The Eton and Harrow match at Lords'," I suggested sarcastically.

"Don't be an ass. Lords'! I keep conjuring up a photograph—Lords'! Don't suppose she's ever heard of Lords' . . . let alone ever been there. . . . Holy Smoke, Bill, I've got it!!! And by a miracle of miracles, your mention of Lords' gave it to me. Great Scott! What a bit of luck."

Now this was the manner of Mr. Bathurst's memory.

"Do you ever see *The Prattler*, Bill?"

"Sometimes! Always when I'm here—Sir Charles Considine has taken it since it started!"

"He has? Better and better, laddie. I'm on the crest of the wave. Listen! This is what I've remembered. Do you remember the second Test Match of the Australian tour in 1921? At Lords'."

"What are you getting at?" I said rather peevishly. "Are you trying to prove that it rained or something—you know it always rains for Test Matches."

"No—I'm deadly serious. The Australians won easily—but that isn't the point—the last ball bowled—by Durston it was, flew out of his hand and went somewhere in the region of 'cover.' Before the umpire called 'wide' Bardsley, who was batting at the time, chased after it, got to it, and promptly 'despatched it to the boundary' as the reporters said. I remember the incident perfectly now." He smiled with satisfaction.

"Well," I said, "What in the name of thunder has this to do with Marshall?"

"This, Bill." His voice grew serious.

"*The Prattler* printed a photograph of the incident. . . ."

"Yes . . ." I remarked.

"And next to the photograph—in the adjoining space—they printed a photograph of *Fraulein Marshall*. Now what do you say? *I can see it now.*"

"In what relation? . . ." I protested.

"Can't recall, William. All I can see is Bardsley's uplifted bat and adjoining it the face of *Marshall*. It's five years ago, remember. But we'll soon find out. It's easy! Or it should be." He sprang to his feet excitedly. "We will now proceed to investigate. I wonder what Sir Charles does with his old *Prattlers*?"

"Best way to find out will be to ask him!" I ventured.

"Excellent advice, William, that I am going to take. *Allons!*" Mary Considine met us as we went up to the house.

She looked deathly pale, I thought, and utterly discomfited by the events of the day. I would much rather have stopped in the garden with Mary than gone chasing old copies of *The Prattler* with Anthony. She stopped us.

"Bill—Mr. Bathurst! I have just been interviewed by Inspector Baddeley, and been asked if I can recognize some handwriting." She flung us a glance under her long lashes. "Tell me," she questioned us, "does he suspect anybody in the house of having done this awful thing? It's unthinkable."

"Don't you worry, Mary," I replied. "It's only the usual official formality carried out by the Police."

She turned to Anthony.

"Who could have killed him, Mr. Bathurst? I can't realize it—yesterday alive and in such . . . good spirits . . . and now to-day. . . ." She broke off and shook her head helplessly.

"You're upset," said Anthony, sympathetically. "Very naturally. It has been a shock to you. How is Lady Considine?"

"Wonderful, considering. I think the murder has to some extent mitigated the loss of her pearls . . . can you understand?" She looked up at him and then half smiled towards me. Her pallor only seemed to accentuate her loveliness. I have never seen eyes like Mary's—and I found myself dreaming dreams.

"Jack has sent word to poor Mrs. Prescott—I don't know what I shall say to her." The violet eyes fringed with tears. "It would have been difficult," she went on, "with someone you knew . . . it will be infinitely more difficult with a stranger."

Anthony conveyed more sympathy with a slight gesture.

"I am sure it will be in able hands. Can you help me now? I want to turn up an old copy of *The Prattler*. Bill tells me your father has taken it for years. Do you keep them?"

"How long ago is the copy you want?"

"Just over five years," he replied.

"Then we can't help you. We never keep more than those of the current year. Is it important?"

"It is, rather," responded Anthony. "Do you know what becomes of them?"

"I am not quite sure, Mr. Bathurst, but I believe Father sends them to the Cottage Hospital. Come in and see Father—he'll tell you at once."

Sir Charles and Lady Considine were in the library.

"Father," said Mary, "Mr. Bathurst and Bill want you. They want to know where the old copies of *The Prattler* go?"

Sir Charles looked wonderment.

"It's rather an unusual request, I know, sir," said Anthony; "but believe me, I have excellent reasons for worrying you over it."

"*The Prattler?* They're sent to the Allingham Cottage Hospital at the end of every year," he said.

"H'm—hard luck," muttered Anthony. "The Allingham Cottage Hospital! Far from here?"

"No," declared Sir Charles. "About five miles, walking across the Downs. Eight and a half by road."

"A walk across the Downs would be the very thing for Bill . . . he shall have it. He shall accompany me."

"Which I hope will prove to be the end of a perfect day," I grumbled.

"You look pretty tired, Bill, now I can gaze upon you properly," he said, as we struck off across the Downs. "But I shan't be able to rest till I've satisfied myself. Till then my eager excitement will keep me going."

"I am tired," I rejoined. "And I've a very shrewd idea that we are on a fool's errand. I don't suppose for one moment they keep copies of periodicals for five years."

"Very likely you're right, Bill. It's a long shot, but it may strike home—there's nothing lost if we don't—we can easily turn up the files at the British Museum—but that will take time—whereas this is opportune."

After about one hour and a quarter's walking, we saw our objective. Anthony gave his card to the porter and after a brief period of waiting we were ushered into the presence of the Matron.

The atmosphere of Considine Manor worked wonders. I have always noticed that the Matron dearly loves a lord.

She could not say if she could help Mr. . . . she referred to his card . . . Mr. Bathurst . . . many periodicals and magazines were presented to the Hospital . . . but she didn't know quite what became of them. She would ring for the steward. Anthony thanked her. Yes, the steward could help us. Most of the books of that kind when finished with, were sold to a man named Clarke, who kept a shop in Brighton.

"What kind of a shop?" asked Anthony.

"A kind of second-hand bookseller's, where old magazines and periodicals of all kinds were put in boxes in front of the shop and sold for twopence or threepence."

"Hopeless, Bill. Perfectly hopeless!" He turned to express his thanks.

The Matron expressed her sorrow that his quest was fruitless.

Then the steward of the Allingham Cottage Hospital had a brain-wave.

"It's just come to me, sir," he exclaimed, "that Dr. Macken-zie—that's the doctor in the village—used to take *The Prattler* to put on the table of his waiting-room. He's a lot of office patients, you see, sir, and isn't over particular about the date of the news he puts in front of them. So he may have some old ones."

"It's a chance, certainly," exclaimed Anthony, "but a slen-der one.

"Thank you, Matron. Now for Dr. Mackenzie. There are points in favour of his parsimony."

The steward directed us, and ten minutes' quick walk brought us to the house. The doctor was in. He listened to us . . . would be pleased to help us. As far as he knew all the *Spears* were somewhere in the Office Patients' waiting-room . . . yes, and *The Prattlers*. Would we care to look? There would be a couple of dozen or so on the table—the rest would be in a pile on a book wagon there. . . .

"June, Bill . . ." muttered Anthony. "About the third week in June."

It was not on the table. I wasn't sorry . . . too greasy and too well-thumbed to be exactly pleasant. We divided the piles from the wagon. About twenty each. An exclamation from Anthony!

"Here it is, Bill. This would be the one. Come and look."

He turned the pages rapidly . . . then. . . .

"There!" triumphantly, "look at that."

I looked.

There was the Test Match photograph he had described to me, and next to it, just as he had said, was the face of Marshall, and underneath it I was amazed to read—"Constance Webb, wife of 'Spider' Webb, the famous jewel thief of three coun-tries, leaving the Central Criminal Court, at the conclusion of her husband's trial. He was sentenced to five years' penal servitude."

## CHAPTER IX

# MR. BATHURST CALLS UPON THE POSTMISTRESS

"Good Lord!" I exclaimed. "That settles it. A topping shot of yours, Anthony!"

"Not so bad," he admitted. "But not exactly a shot—I remembered the face and the associations. Spare my blushes."

"Ole Baddeley will listen with both ears when you show him this," I continued. "In a way I'm glad it's turned out like this . . . it was a pretty ghastly thought to imagine that anybody in the house could have been the guilty party. But this settles it."

"Settles what, Bill?"

"Why—the affair—Prescott of course! Why do you ask?"

Anthony shook his head. "On the contrary, Bill, this settles two little matters but *not*, distinctly *not*, the affair of Prescott as you call it. I don't like to think about that too much. There, Bill, as the immortal Sherlock would say, 'we are in very deep waters.'"

Dr. Mackenzie joined us. Had we had any success . . . yes? . . . he was gratified. . . .

"May I take this copy of *The Prattler* with me, Doctor?" said Anthony. "I shall be happy to recompense you for its loss."

"Certainly not! I couldn't hear of it," said the doctor. He would have liked us to have stayed for dinner, but he was very much afraid that his *cuisine* might not be adequate!

"Many thanks, Doctor,"—Anthony with one of his rare smiles—"we understand perfectly. Besides, we are anxious to get back. Good-afternoon."

I harked back directly we were outside the house.

"I should be eternally obliged if you would explain things a bit, old man," I declared, a trifle resentfully. "Surely this clears things up considerably."

"This clears the robbery problem—Lady Considine's robbery—and it effectively explains that very vexed question that bothered a number of us—why Marshall opened the window. Beyond that—"

"Tell me," I begged.

"Well, it's pretty evident that Marshall took the case containing the pearl necklace from Lady Considine's bedroom, and it's also fairly conclusive that she conveyed that same case to her husband—'Spider' Webb—via the window of the billiard room. The second set of footprints we shall very soon discover to be that august gentleman's. And I think they were the footsteps that Dick and Helen Arkwright heard. But I don't think . . ." he paused and reflected.

"You don't think what?"

"I don't think it was the billiard room door that Jack Considine fancies he heard shutting." He slashed with his stick at the grass as we walked.

"Was it Prescott's door?" I broke in eagerly. "Did Prescott hear anything and come down to meet his death?"

My theory excited me.

"No, Bill, I don't think so. All my intuition and instinct, if you care to call it that, lead me away from that idea."

"What about Marshall—or Mrs. Spider as she is—and the window? You haven't explained that yet," I insisted, "properly!"

"Prescott's body on the billiard-table was an overwhelming surprise to Marshall when she opened the door this morning. She had dropped the 'sparklers,' as Comrade Spider probably calls them, out of the window and closed it again. Then gone quietly back to bed in the servants' part of the house. Now for her surprise! When she enters the room a few hours later she comes face to face with a greater and more sinister crime. She at once, in her mind, connects the two things! Had 'Spider' come back for anything, encountered Prescott and killed him? Had they fought? Was 'Spider' hurt? She had last seen him just outside the window. Was he there still, wounded perhaps? She rushes to the window and flings it open. *Voilà*, Bill!"

I nodded in approval. Yet—

"Where does Prescott come in then?" I queried. "Did he meet Webb *outside*?"

Anthony stopped and looked at me.

"That's an idea. I never considered that. Outside! That's certainly a possibility."

"One more point," I said, secretly pleased to have set him thinking, "and that may be two . . . apparently nothing else has been stolen besides Lady Considine's necklace . . . that is to say nothing in the jewel line. . . . How comes the Venetian dagger to be in the billiard room?" Anthony looked grave.

"That's a poser," he commented. "But it must not be forgotten that we are dealing with two adventures . . . 'The Adventure of Lady Considine's Necklace' and 'The Adventure of the Death in the Billiard Room' . . . there may be no connection whatever between the two . . . and yet, as you have suggested, Bill, there may."

"The Venetian dagger was always kept in the drawing-room," I maintained. "Therefore, the person that took it, *went* to the drawing-room to get it."

"True . . . but when? That's the point. Also, Bill, why was the dagger used when Prescott was already dead—strangled?"

"Perhaps the murderer didn't know he was dead. Now I'm coming to that second point at which I hinted just now . . . something I fail to understand at all. How do you account for the absence of blood stains? As far as I could see, Prescott lay on the billiard-table on his shoulder, there was no blood on the table, though, and his clothing seemed to show very little trace. . . . I should have imagined, though I don't pretend to know, that a blow struck with the force that that had been would have caused a rush of blood from the wound."

Anthony nodded. "Good for you—the same feature struck me—but Dr. Elliot had an explanation. He says that a blow struck at the top of the spinal cord as this blow was, produced, in a living body, almost an instantaneous paralysis, and that he would expect, as a medical man, a very small quantity of blood to be shed. This was a dead body when the blow was struck, remember! But why the dagger was ever used . . . well, I'm in considerable doubt."

"And I," I rejoined. "And I can't see much hope of our doubts being dispelled."

Anthony looked at his wrist watch.

"We've got time to go home through the village," he said. "I want to make a call."

"Are you going to tell Baddeley of this Marshall business at once?" I asked. "He can't very well arrest her because she's the wife of a man who was sentenced for jewel robbery five years ago."

"It would be taking a chance, wouldn't it?" he grinned.

"It wouldn't surprise me if she hasn't cleared by now," I said, reflectively. "You shook her up a bit this morning."

"All the better if she has . . . but she hasn't, you'll find."

"Why?"

"If she's cleared, Baddeley's men will have shadowed her . . . and she'll lead them straight to the 'Spider'" . . . he thought for a moment. "Still, I've an idea that she'll let me know where he is when we've talked to her for a little while."

By this time we had reached the village and coming down the hill from the track that leads from the Downs, we entered the main street.

"I am of the opinion, Bill," said Anthony, "that a few discreet inquiries here may prove of interest and advantage. I suggest that we call and see Mrs. Hogarth at the Post Office. Does she know you, Bill?"

"She remembers me as a guest at the Manor for some years, at any rate," I responded.

"That's the stuff to give 'em,"—Anthony waxed merry—"I want her to talk and tell us things—if she knows you it will help tremendously."

The Post Office was a "general" shop that sold everything from pins to Postal Orders.

"See that?" murmured Anthony, as we entered, heralded by the loud clanging of the shop bell on the door. He pointed to the telephone call-box. "I hoped that the 'phone would be in here."

Mrs. Hogarth bustled out.

He nudged me in the ribs. "Introduce yourself—tell her who you are."

"Good-afternoon, Mrs. Hogarth," I cried with an air. "How's the rheumatism?"

"Why, it's Mr. Cunningham from the Manor. Good-afternoon, sir. The rheumatics? . . . oh, not so bad, sir, considering
my age and all that . . . this is a terrible thing I hear, sir, what's
happened up at the Manor!"

"Yes, Mrs. Hogarth," I replied. "It is! This is Mr. Bathurst, a
very intimate friend of Sir Charles and her Ladyship—"

Mrs. Hogarth curtsied to the best of her ability—"Pleased to
meet you, sir—"

"And they would be glad," I continued, "if you would give
him any information for which he may ask you."

"Only too pleased, Mr. Cunningham."

"Thank you," said Anthony, "I shan't worry you unduly. This
'phone call-box" . . . he motioned towards it . . . "is this the nearest one to Considine Manor?"

"Oh yes, sir. By far. The next one is almost to Allingham . . .
a matter of close on six miles."

"Now quite in confidence, Mrs. Hogarth, in the very strict-
est confidence, Sir Charles Considine has asked me to conduct
a little inquiry on his behalf. And he suggests that first of all I
should come and see you."

Mrs. Hogarth's excitement increased. "You may rely on me,
sir. . . ."

"I'm sure I can," exclaimed Anthony. "Now my real question
is this . . . do you know one of the maids at present employed at
Considine Manor, of the name of Marshall?"

"Why, yes, sir, and it's a funny thing her name should have
left your lips so soon after you asking me about that there telephone it is."

"Oh? Why is that, Mrs. Hogarth?" smiled Anthony. "Has she
been using it lately?"

"As sure as I stand here, sir, she was the very last person to
do so."

"This is very interesting, Mrs. Hogarth . . . very interesting,
and I must congratulate you on your excellent memory. You are
quite certain of your statement?"

"Positive, sir! You see, it's like this. We're a small village
here, as you might say, comparatively speaking that is, and most

of the telephone custom we get is from the betting people—there are the Lewes and Brighton bookies you see—so I get to know the regular customers and just about when to expect them—which is from about half-past twelve till about four o'clock—and not so very many after dinner at that—see? Well, yesterday morning, about a quarter past eleven, the bell rings and I bustles out . . . only to find it's a 'phone call. I could see a female in the box which was a bit unusual at that time o' day, as I've said . . . so I waited for her to come out . . . as you might say . . . when she did, who should I set my eyes on but Marshall, the maid from the Manor?"

"Of course you couldn't hear anything of the message?" inquired Anthony.

Mrs. Hogarth shook her head. "No, sir, I couldn't . . . and I ain't the sort to listen hard!"

Anthony accepted her denial with a disarming smile.

"Of course not, Mrs. Hogarth, Mr. Cunningham and I are fully alive to that. Did she appear agitated at all?"

Mrs. Hogarth pursed her lips and pondered for a moment.

"No, sir, I wouldn't say that. Yet she had a look on her that's hard to describe." She pondered still more.

"Yes," said Anthony, encouragingly, "perhaps I can help you . . . eh? She looked pleased with herself, didn't she?"

Mrs. Hogarth knocked the counter with the palm of her hand.

"That's it, sir, that's it . . . her face was hot, as you might say, flushed you might call it, with pleasure. That was a extryordin-ary good guess, sir." Mrs. Hogarth was in the seventh heaven of delight—she had assisted this friend of Sir Charles Considine, she felt sure. She would now fire her last shot, her crowning triumph.

"There's one other little thing, sir, now I come to think of it," she murmured with more than a suggestion of an apology in her tone, "I wasn't listening to the conversation in any way, sir, I know my place here better than to do that, but I've just an idea that I did just manage to hear the last sentence the hussy spoke." She breathed heavily as she looked at us.

"Better and better, Mrs. Hogarth," said Anthony. "You're a veritable 'Treasure-Trove' of information. Let's hear it."

"Well, sir, as she was a-finishing the conversation she was having, I'm almost sure I overheard her say 'Good-bye, Emma!'"

"Thank you, Mrs. Hogarth. Nothing more?"

"No sir, I couldn't remember anything else."

"I needn't trouble you any more, then. You have helped me considerably. Come along, Bill." We bowed ourselves out, personally conducted by the postmistress—a beaming postmistress now—and started homeward.

"Well, Bill, things are plainer now with a vengeance," said Anthony decisively. . . . "I think if I put these facts before Baddeley he will take action . . . if necessary the call should be easy to trace . . . then Webb can be taken comfortably."

"The Spider?" I queried.

He assented. "They call him 'Spider' as much for his physical as for the name association," he continued. "I remember seeing his photo when he was tried and sentenced—he has long thin arms and long thin legs—with smallish feet."

"What was the 'phone message?" I asked.

"That she had the pearls, laddie! She has been planted there to get them . . . the 'Spider' flies high . . . or shall we say he spins high . . . forged references doubtless . . . she waited three years for her chance. Yesterday it came. Her 'phone message to the 'Spider' was 'Success' with a capital 'S,' William! Best part of the three years he's been in prison."

"You don't know she did 'phone her husband," I ventured, with criticism in my voice. "Why call him Emma? It may have been the most harmless of conversations."

"No, Bill—all your wonted eloquence will not convince me of that. She 'phoned the 'Spider,' informing him of her luck. 'I've got the necklace,' she said, 'when are you coming for it?' Shall I go on with the conversation, Bill?"

"Please do," I said mockingly and a little incredulously.

"Well 'Spider' probably said, 'Where shall I come?' The reply was 'outside the billiard room' . . . directions how to find it followed . . . then arose the question of time. Listening, Bill?"

I grinned. "Carry on . . . I don't say I believe it all though."

"I repeat it, Bill . . . then came the question of timing the assignation. It had to be after dark . . . she couldn't get away during dinner, for instance, her absence would have been detected instantly, and she couldn't risk the garden after dinner, there was always the chance of guests going there . . . Jack Considine and I were there, for example, so she had to wait till all was quiet. Now when would that be, William?"

"Oh," I replied, "somewhere about one o'clock in the morning, I suppose, at the earliest."

"Exactly," responded Anthony nonchalantly. "Sometime, we will say about one, or possibly two—'ack Emma!' S'that—Umpire? Is it a hit?"

I gasped! And I had completely missed that meaning—plain as a pike staff now I had secured the explanation.

"Not so bad, Bill, eh?" muttered Anthony quizzically. "Don't overwhelm me with your admiration."

"You're a perishin' marvel," I said—"I never thought of that—I shouldn't have expected Marshall to use the term, for one thing."

"'Spider' probably saw Service," he replied—"she has picked it up from him. That's the solution of that. Here we are—now for friend Baddeley."

"You don't think then," I said, "that we are nearing the finish of the Prescott affair?"

"As I told you before, Bill, no! I shall see Baddeley now, put these discoveries in front of him, let him act on them . . . he'll be delighted to . . . it will save his face, temporarily at least . . . then I shall turn my attention to the more complex problem . . . which I think will prove to be very dark and very sinister. Certainly, the latter."

I searched his face with my eyes, but gathered nothing from the inspection. It was heavy and troubled, but the clouds soon passed. Anthony Bathurst was like that, mood succeeded mood very rapidly. In the Hall we encountered Roper. He had a message for us from Baddeley.

"The Inspector has had the body removed to the mortuary, gentlemen," he said, "and would like you to. . . ."

Anthony cut into his speech—"Where is the Inspector? . . . I should like a word with him immediately . . . if possible. Will you find him and tell him?" Roper departed on his errand.

"Take a pew, Bill," said Anthony, "and watch for his face to light up."

Baddeley was quickly with us.

"Yes, Mr. Bathurst, Roper here tells me you want me." He looked at us with an air of inquiry.

"I have some information for you, Inspector," commenced Anthony as coolly as possible, "that may help you considerably towards the recovery of Lady Considine's necklace, and the arrest of the thief."

Baddeley favoured him with a steady and sustained stare.

"The deuce you have," he exclaimed.

"I had an advantage over you, you see," proceeded Anthony—"in the fact that Marshall's face seemed familiar to me and awakened a memory in me that I have been able to follow up." He paused and then continued with deliberation . . . "to follow up successfully." He opened *The Prattler.*

"Look at that, will you, Inspector? And gain enlightenment."

Baddeley bent down in amazement. "By Moses!" he yelled . . . "that's she . . . a guinea to a gooseberry on it. Smart work, Mr. Bathurst. I'm grateful, sir, for the hint." He wrung Anthony's hand. Anthony laughed.

"We can get this Webb, I think, Baddeley; . . . listen." He recounted the evidence of Mrs. Hogarth.

Baddeley was respectfully attentive. "You haven't let the grass grow under your feet, that's a sure thing," he declared.

Anthony smiled again. "And I don't suppose you have either, Inspector, if the truth's known."

Baddeley grimaced.

"What do you mean, sir, exactly by that remark?" he queried.

"I can't forget," pronounced Anthony, "that there are two most important things still missing: the Barker I.O.U. and the shoe-lace that killed Prescott."

# CHAPTER X
# WALK INTO MY PARLOUR

BADDELEY acquiesced. "That's very true. And the more I see of the case, the more I—Still, let's deal with the matter in hand. There isn't a reasonable doubt, Mr. Bathurst, that you've put your hooks into the right people for this jewel robbery. And one thing at a time, say I."

Anthony bowed to the compliment. "We can get 'Spider' Webb easily enough," he said, "in any one of half a dozen ways. We'll discuss that in a few moments. I'm more concerned about Lady Considine's chance of getting her pearls back. How do we stand there?" The Inspector thought for a moment.

"Let's see. They were taken in the early hours of this morning. To-morrow's Sunday. If we can collar our man within twenty-four hours or so we should be able to salve the spoils. Pearls, you see, are different from silver stuff, for example—that's in the pot before you can wink an eye. The best market for what he's got away with might be Amsterdam . . . he'd probably try about the beginning of next week."

"Right!" exclaimed Anthony. "I'm inclined to agree with you. Now, how about getting our man? Is it worth while following up Marshall's telephone call?"

"I've got a better plan than that, Mr. Bathurst. You wait and see and let me know what you think of it. I've had Marshall under observation since this morning . . ." he grinned as though the reflection afforded him some amusement . . . "as a matter of fact ever since I first arrived—although I admit you were a step ahead of me over that window business . . . and she's made no attempt at communication with anybody. She's cute enough to realize that her best plan is to say and do nothing: just go about her ordinary daily duties as though nothing had happened. Also she's scared stiff about the murder." He glanced at us both . . . almost as though he wanted us to confirm his opinion.

Then I butted in. "You're satisfied then, Inspector, that Webb didn't murder Prescott—despite all this evidence?"

Anthony looked searchingly at Baddeley. The Inspector's face grew grim and hard. But he found time to answer me although I had half-suspected that he would evade the question. He chose his words carefully.

"Not despite—because of—the evidence, Mr. Cunningham!" He turned to Anthony with the same kind of look as before, but Anthony remained silent. I got the impression that Baddeley would have liked to make him talk, and that Anthony knew it.

"We'll have her in here, Mr. Bathurst." He went to the door and called Roper.

"Bring that maid Marshall in here, Roper. Don't tell her anything—don't even say who it is wants to speak to her."

Marshall came, shepherded by Roper. She was very white, but still held her head high with a sort of impudent defiance.

"Sit down there," said Baddeley, motioning her to a chair. "I've sent for you because I want you to pass on a little useful information. Got that?"

She tossed her head back. "I've told you all I know, Inspector, and that being so, I can't very well tell you any more," and a bright red spot blazed in her white cheek.

Baddeley waved her protestations on one side. Here he was sure of himself, certain of what he was going to do, confident of ultimate success.

"There's one piece of information you can give me, my girl, and that dead smart, so make up your mind on that," he rapped. "You might as well know now as later . . . the game's up!!"

Marshall gasped, and her hand went to her throat . . . help-lessly.

"Where's 'Spider' Webb to be found these days?" roared Baddeley. "Eh—*Mrs.* Webb?"

She gazed at him affrighted, wild-eyed, with bosom heaving. Then summoned sufficient desperation to her aid to make one last attempt at fight. "I don't know what you—"

"Cut that," broke in the Inspector, "that won't get you anything. We know you . . . we know him . . . we know your little lay in the billiard room last night when you handed over the Considine pearls. *Where is he?*"

"That I'll never tell you," she retorted—"never!"

"I think you will, my lady, when you've heard all I have to say," stormed Baddeley, "if you don't help me all you can and come across with what you know, I'll do my level best to 'swing' your pretty 'Spider.'"

Her face went ashen, and as the full import of his speech reached her brain, horror tinged her features.

"You can't!" she gasped. "You can't! The 'Spider' never touched 'im, never saw 'im . . . the room was empty when I left it . . . the 'Spider' went . . . it's God's own truth I'm telling you. . . ."

"I want the truth," went on Baddeley, remorselessly and relentlessly, "you tell the truth and help me . . . and I'll help you . . . if I can, that is."

"It *is* the truth," she sobbed. "The 'Spider' wouldn't 'urt a fly."

"No, I know, it doesn't sound as though he would," said Baddeley derisively. "Spiders don't, as a rule, do they? You're trapped, my girl, and you'll see the inside of a prison cell before supper time to-night . . . you realize that, don't you? . . . and if you don't tell me where this precious husband of yours is to be found . . . well, I shall find him all the same, and it will go pretty hard with the pair of you," he paused, and then proceeded with studied deliberation, "ten years for you, we'll say, and the execution shed for your partner."

She gazed at him—fascinated at the dreadful picture he had painted for her imagination to dwell upon. Then answered him, white-lipped and trembling.

"I'll tell you the truth," she murmured. "Then you'll know my 'usband couldn't 'ave done that awful thing. I took the necklace from Lady Considine's room as I 'ad meant to do . . . I come into this 'ouse to get it . . . I 'ad to wait a long time for my chance . . . but it come yesterday . . . I saw it laying on the dressing-table and took it. Then I arranged for the 'Spider' to come for it so's I shouldn't be suspected and about two o'clock this morning I dropped it to 'im from the billiard room window. In ten minutes at the most 'e 'ad gone. It's the solemn truth, Inspector," she wiped tears from her eyes, "if I never speak another word, and when I got down there first thing this morning, and there was that corpse on the table—you could 'ave knocked me down with a feather."

"H'm! That's all very well. But how do you know your husband didn't come back for something—something that he'd dropped, perhaps—and met Mr. Prescott who challenged him?"

She shook her head. "'E didn't—'e didn't. 'E just went at once!"

"You don't know," reiterated Baddeley. "He may have come back, run into Mr. Prescott, struggled with him and killed him. You don't know, so you can't say."

"I know I don't," she muttered piteously—"but 'e didn't. It wouldn't be like him to do no such thing."

"Then what did you open the window for?" cut in Baddeley decisively—"you had doubts yourself as to what had happened after you left the billiard room."

The fight was all gone from her now. "Yes," she said. "I was frightened. I worried about what I knew 'ad 'appened. All the same my 'usband never touched 'im—I'll take my dying oath on that." She looked sullenly in front of her.

"Where is he, then?" Then as no answer was forthcoming, "Good Lord, girl, we'll get him right enough, whether you tell us or not . . . make no mistake about that . . . it's merely a question of time . . . but, mark my words . . . the sooner he tells the truth about the robbery . . . the more chance he has of clearing himself with regard to the murder."

Marshall made as if to speak, but hesitated.

Baddeley saw the advantage he had gained and hastened to follow it up. "The sooner we get to work while the scent is hot, the greater likelihood of finding the murderer," he said, with decision in his tone. "Come, my girl, that must be as plain to you as the nose on my face."

She hesitated again, and twisted her hands nervously in her lap.

"I don't know what to do," she moaned. "You're asking me to betray my 'usband—and if I do, it's only to save 'im from something worse—but it's prison for me, and prison for 'im at the best of things."

"That's so," declared Baddeley mercilessly, "but a 'stretch' is better than the gallows."

"May I be forgiven then," said Marshall—"you'll find the 'Spider' at 45, Peabody Buildings, Poplar. And for mercy's sake, don't let 'im know who told you."

Baddeley motioned to Roper. "Get her down to the station, Roper . . . I'll be down later."

"We must tell Sir Charles, Inspector," said Anthony, as Roper departed with his charge. "I haven't mentioned this latest development to him . . . I came straight to you with the news."

"Naturally," rejoined Baddeley, "naturally. We'll ask him to step this way. Do you mind, Mr. Cunningham?"

I found the old man in the garden with Mary. The trouble of the whole affair was just beginning to show on their faces. . . . Considine Manor had by this time become the talk of thousands. Mary seemed very grief-laden . . . they turned as I approached.

I gave him Baddeley's message.

"Certainly, Bill, I'll come in at once. Is there news, then?"

"Rather," I replied. "Come and hear what Baddeley has to say."

"What is it, Bill?" asked Mary, eagerly.

"Can't tell you yet," I whispered evasively, "but we're on the track of the pearls—anyway!"

"This is extraordinarily good news," said Sir Charles, as we went into the house. "How did Baddeley manage it?"

"It was Bathurst," I replied. "You'll hear what they have to say—and you'll get a bit of a shock."

He looked at me curiously. "Don't be alarmed," I said. "Nothing to worry about."

"Thank you, Bill. To tell the truth you did startle me a bit . . . I began to wonder . . ." he wiped his forehead . . . "it's been a day of surprises."

Baddeley speedily described our discoveries (I say "our") and the result thereof. Sir Charles gasped.

"Marshall!" he exclaimed incredulously. "You astound me. And she came with such splendid references. Well, well, well, truly one never knows. My wife's pearls, Inspector. Do you think there's any probability of restoring them? You've done so splendidly that one becomes quite optimistic." His eyes gleamed. "And you say you don't really connect the affair with poor young Prescott?"

"At the moment, Sir Charles, I'm not inclined to link up the two . . . and as for your praises"—he turned towards Anthony—"it's Mr. Bathurst here that put me on the track."

Anthony laughed. "Proving my theories, Sir Charles, that's all! And I was lucky."

"Well, I congratulate you then, as a combination—we'll leave it at that. By the way, Baddeley, you didn't answer me about the pearls. What do you really think?"

"I'm going to put a suggestion in front of you directly, Sir Charles, that will answer that question for you. Have most of your guests gone?"

"Yes, Inspector; as sanctioned by you, after your little round of interrogations this morning, they have all departed for their homes. No good purpose could have been served by their staying. I have a list of their present addresses for you. Mr. Cunningham and Mr. Bathurst, and my daughter and son-in-law, Mr. and Mrs. Arkwright, will stay on. That is to say, for a time. Well, Fitch, what is it?"

The butler had approached him.

"Your pardon, Sir Charles, but there's a newspaper man here wishes to speak to you. Here's his card."

Sir Charles took it. "Sydney Dennison. *The Morning Message*. A London reporter, gentlemen," he announced. "Shall I? . . ."

Baddeley cut in. "Have him in, Sir Charles, won't do any harm."

A fresh-faced young fellow came in and bowed to us.

"Sorry to disturb you gentlemen, but I've motored down from London. . . . Can you give me any details of what has taken place here?"

Baddeley briefly recounted the affair, but withheld all details relevant to the arrest of Marshall.

"Murder and robbery then as we were informed on the 'phone by our local agent," said Dennison. "Any arrest imminent?"

The Inspector took a moment or two to answer. "I am holding a person," he replied slowly, "on the robbery charge only, so far, but I should be very much obliged, Mr. Dennison, and it will, I think, assist me considerably, if you make no mention of the arrest whatever. That is to say, yet awhile."

Dennison's eyes went up in interrogation.

"I will promise you," proceeded Baddeley, "that no other paper gets the information to publish before you. I shall certainly see to that."

"You think it will assist? . . ." queried Dennison.

"I think it will assist the cause of justice," said Baddeley gravely.

"That's why you ask me?"

"That's why I ask you!"

"Right you are, Inspector. I will finish my report for *The Message*, by saying for the time being, the Police are entirely without a clue—eh?"

"Nothing would please me better," said Baddeley, rubbing his palms together.

"I understand perfectly." Dennison rose to depart. He had his story and in a few days would have a still better one. "Now for London again."

"One moment," cried the Inspector. "One more thing. I would like the bewilderment of the Police to appear in the late edition of your *Evening Gazette*. That all right? That will be better still."

"As you wish, Inspector, and thank you. Good-bye!" And in a brief period we heard the sound of his motorcycle en route for headquarters again. Press methods are short and sharp.

Baddeley turned to us and although he addressed us as a company, the feeling persisted in me that Anthony was his audience as far as he himself was concerned.

"That brings me, gentlemen, to the matter of the 'Spider.' We've got to get him, and we ought to get him at once . . . while,

I think, the pearls are *on* him . . . before he takes a little trip somewhere."

"We know where he is?" interjected Sir Charles.

"Yes," continued Baddeley, "but I don't purpose going there for him."

"Where, then?" I interposed.

"Well, this is my plan. Get the 'Spider' back here—then take him. It has the merits of simplicity and comfort." He smiled.

"Mahomet and the mountain, eh?" smiled Anthony.

"Something like it," answered the Inspector.

"But will he come?" demanded Sir Charles. "It appears to me to be extremely doubtful. Would any criminal walk into an obvious trap like that? . . . You're expecting too much, Baddeley."

"I don't think so, Sir Charles, if you'll allow me to say so. If, as I think and I fancy as Mr. Bathurst here, thinks, the murder of Mr. Prescott is a complete surprise to the 'Spider,' then it's given him a pretty nasty shock . . . he's wondering, gentlemen, wondering very considerably. And he will see in the late editions of the London papers this evening that the Police are completely in the dark . . . so he won't be dreaming any bad dreams himself . . . yet awhile . . . but he'll still go on wondering. Now, I think, gentlemen, that my idea will bring him along quite comfortably. I'm going to telegraph to him like this. 'Come—same place—same time—urgent!'"

"Whom from?" interposed Anthony. "Who's the sender?"

"That I admit, Mr. Bathurst, is its weakness. If I get hold of his wife's Christian name, it's just possible I might use the wrong form or the wrong abbreviation . . . familiar names are awkward things to take chances with in messages—a man calls his wife by a nickname, perhaps—still . . ." he paused and drummed with his hands on the table, reflecting. "How about putting Marshall?"

None of us answered. I think we were all engaged in weighing up the advisability.

Baddeley went on. "If it's unusual for her to send to him under that name, he may think she has a special reason in light of what's happened after the burglary. Whereas, if, for instance, her name's 'Kate' and I put 'Katie' when the 'Spider' always knows her as 'Kitty'—it's bound to create doubt and suspicion."

Anthony sat thinking. "I'm disposed to agree with you, Inspector," he said.

"You think it's worth trying, Mr. Bathurst?" asked Sir Charles.

"Yes, I do." Baddeley seemed pleased. "Get that telegram off then. Roper will take it for us . . . he should be back by now. But perhaps I'd better go and see."

"What about to-night then, Inspector?" said Anthony. "What time shall we gather around to receive our guest? Just after twelve?"

Baddeley rubbed his chin with his forefinger.

"I don't think we'll take any chances, Mr. Bathurst, so we had better be in our places by midnight. He's an awkward customer, there's no doubt about that, this 'Spider' Webb, so if you've a revolver it might come in useful. I'll bring along a couple of men from the station, so with Roper and Mr. Cunningham, there'll be half a dozen of us. We mustn't let him slip through our fingers."

Sir Charles looked grave. "I'll trust there will be no shooting, Inspector. Lady Considine is sufficiently upset already without . . ." he looked at Baddeley with anxiety.

The Inspector pursed his lips together. "I'm sorry, Sir Charles, I fully realize all that . . . but I want this man badly . . . and I don't think, if my plan goes smoothly, that there will be any noise worth worrying about." Sir Charles nodded.

"And what's more," proceeded Baddeley, "I'm pretty confident he'll have the pearls with him. It's worth the risk, you see, sir."

Sir Charles appeared more reconciled.

"Very well then, and may you be successful." He bowed himself out.

"I'll get down to Roper, then," said Baddeley to us, "and get this wire off. Then I'll meet you gentlemen here at eleven-thirty this evening. We'll have five men in the grounds—including both of you—and in the meantime, I'll think out the best disposition of my forces . . ." he grinned at us.

"I thought you said six men, just now, Inspector," I ventured.

"I did," he replied. "The sixth will be in the billiard room, of course."

"You forget, Bill," chuckled Anthony, "Inspector Baddeley is 'marshalling' his forces."

Baddeley burst into hearty laughter. "Very good, Mr. Bathurst, very good." He waved his hand to us. "Till eleven-thirty then."

"Will the 'Spider' come, Anthony?" I asked.

He thought for a moment before replying—"I think he will. Curiosity is a tremendous impetus. I think he will. And of course, he's got to think of his own neck so he must be kept well posted. He'll think his wife has important news for him."

"Good," I cried. "Welcome to the 'Spider'!"

"Yes," said Anthony. "Somewhere about one-thirty, I imagine. And we'll welcome him with this." He fingered his automatic. "If necessary."

## CHAPTER XI
## WHAT WAS FOUND ON THE "SPIDER"

PUNCTUALLY at eleven-thirty, Baddeley and Roper arrived at the Manor. They joined us in the library. Sir Charles was worried and fidgety. "The ladies have gone to bed," he volunteered the information. "Let's hope they all sleep well. I'm going to stay in here."

"Very good, Sir Charles," remarked Baddeley. "That was going to be my own proposition. Now we haven't got a great deal of time before getting to our posts. You two gentlemen," he turned to Anthony and me, "will come into the garden and I will join you. We'll get whatever cover we can as near the billiard room as possible—Roper will be in the billiard room itself, and will open it when the right moment comes. My other two men will command the exit if he breaks through the three of us and gets away. A contingency I'm prepared to lay very heavy odds against, though. Revolver all serene, Mr. Bathurst?"

"All in order, Inspector," answered Anthony cheerfully, tapping his pocket. "Do I shoot to kill?"

"Only as a last resource, sir. Come along. And you, Roper, get upstairs to the billiard room."

We emerged into the grounds. It was a wonderful July night. The sky with its clusters of shimmering stars seemed too serene, too majestic, for any disturbance such as our adventure might prove to be.

Baddeley gave a low whistle and, seemingly from nowhere, two plain-clothes men materialized from the shadows. He whispered them their instructions and they departed as quickly and as quietly as they had come.

"Now, Mr. Bathurst," he came across to us as silently as a cat, "what about that rhododendron clump?" He pointed to a spot about eight yards from the window. "We three can make for there."

As we nestled into its shade I heard the village clocks striking twelve. I wondered how many more times I should hear them strike before our vigil ended.

Baddeley gripped my arm. "Don't speak, gentlemen," he whispered, "it's a dead still night, and the sound of the voice carries so. Be as quiet as you can." I nodded to show him I understood and would obey.

It was, as Baddeley had said, as still as death. Occasionally came the hoot of an owl, but beyond that, the only sound that reached my ears was the breathing of my two companions. Baddeley spoke again. "We'd better not smoke," he said. "He might easily detect it as he comes up and you can bet your life he'll come with his eyes skinned." We reluctantly put our pipes away. The minutes passed with unrelenting slowness. Once there came a sudden swishing sound followed by a soft thud. The sweat stood on my brow as I watched the place from where the noise had come, and Anthony gripped my right arm hard. Baddeley smiled at us out of the darkness. "A cat," he whispered—"that's all." Half-past twelve, a quarter to one, and one o'clock struck. Then a quarter past one.

"He isn't coming," I breathed in Anthony's ear. Baddeley looked perturbed and glanced at his watch. "Nearly half-past one," he muttered softly.

"How long will you wait?" I asked him.

"Don't know . . . s'sh. What's that?"

An owl hooted twice in quick succession. Baddeley put his finger to his lips. We waited spellbound. Then, as we watched, we saw a slim dark figure slink down the garden, leave the path leading to the drawing-room windows and come noiselessly up the gravel path. Opposite the billiard room window he stopped, then picked his way quickly and carefully across the bed till he reached the wall below the window. Looking round cautiously he bent down, picked up a handful of earth and threw it sharply against the pane. We saw the window raised slowly and the figure outside watching it.

"Now," said Baddeley. "We'll take him with his back towards us."

Anthony drew his revolver, and we hurled ourselves at the crouching figure. He was utterly and completely taken by surprise.

"Curse you!" he snarled. "What's the game?" But Baddeley silenced him with a buffet to the mouth while Anthony and I flung ourselves upon him. The scuffle was sharp but short. Three against one is merciless odds, and each one of us was bigger than our quarry. A few ineffective kicks and he lay helpless on the ground. Baddeley clicked the bracelets on his wrists.

"Now, Mr. 'Spider' Webb," he cried, "I charge you with the robbery, last night, or to be precise, yesterday morning, of Lady Considine's pearls, and I warn you that anything you say may be used as evidence against you. Bring him inside, gentlemen." He called to Roper. "Tell those other two it's all right—they can leave their positions and get back."

We escorted our prisoner to the library, and on the way I was able to get my first good look at him. Jack Considine and Arkwright joined us.

He was a thin-faced, slim-limbed man with long black hair under his peaked cap. One of a type that can be seen many times over any day in the East End of London. I could quickly see how he had qualified for his sobriquet of "Spider." His face twitched spasmodically as we marched him into the library.

"A very neat piece of work, Sir Charles," exclaimed Baddeley . . . "very neat and quite according to plan."

Our prisoner flashed a glance full of menace at him, malice and spite flickering over his face unmistakably.

"Wot am I charged with?" he grunted. "Let's hear it again."

"The theft of Lady Considine's pearls," rapped Baddeley.

"Oh! Not cradle-snatching or boot-legging . . . nothing fancy-like?"

"And unless you're very careful," went on the Inspector, "you may find yourself called upon to face an even more serious charge than robbery."

Webb whitened, even under his normal pallor. "What might that be?" he muttered.

"The murder of Mr. Gerald Prescott, at Considine Manor," replied Baddeley with studied deliberation.

"I know nothink about that, guvnor, nothink at all. S'elp me God, I don't."

"You knew of the murder then?" snapped Baddeley. "You aren't surprised?"

"I can read, can't I?" jeered Webb. "I ain't exactly a savage!"

"What have you done with the necklace you took? Got it on you still?"

"Course not. D'ye think I've come passenger's luggage in advance?"

"Run him over, Roper." Roper's search was rapid and thorough.

"Not in any of his pockets, sir," he announced.

"I'll take a chance then," said Baddeley. "Take off his coat and waistcoat." Roper obeyed, throwing them over to Sir Charles who handed them to Arkwright, and I saw a look of desperation flit across the "Spider's" face. Baddeley walked quickly over to him. He passed his fingers carefully across his shirt and then thrust his hand fiercely underneath it. He lugged at something under Webb's armpit and all the malevolence of the underworld was revealed in the "Spider's" eyes as he fell back a pace or two. Baddeley tossed his find on the table. Our eyes sought it greedily.

"There you are, gentlemen," he cried with triumph. "The Considine Necklace, if I am not mistaken."

Sir Charles caught it up. A small oilskin bag with two attachments of tape. He pulled the top open. "I congratulate you most heartily, Inspector Baddeley, the pearls are here." He counted them. "And intact."

The Inspector flushed with pleasure. "Dress him again, Roper," he jerked . . . "and take him along."

Arkwright handed the clothes over.

"Pockets empty?" queried Baddeley. Roper proceeded to examine them. "Packet of cigarette-papers"—he threw them on the table—"box of matches, clasp-knife, nothing else . . . stay though . . ." he plunged his hand into the left-hand jacket pocket. "There's something else here . . ." he said, "tape or something." He drew it out!

We sat and looked dumbfounded. For there, before our eyes, he dangled *a worn brown shoe-lace*!

"By Moses!" yelled the Inspector. "It's our man after all."

Webb looked astounded. "Wot d'ye mean?" he stammered. "Wot are yer drivin' at now?" Baddeley eyed him severely.

"This lace, Webb, where did you get it from?"

"Ask me another," came the reply. "To tell the 'onest truth, guvnor, I never knew it was there. Must be an old 'un I've 'ad in my pocket some time and forgotten. Seems to have poked the breeze up yer though! Am I charged with pinchin' that, too?"

The Inspector's eyes never left Webb's face. "Mr. Gerald Prescott, a guest here of Sir Charles Considine, was found murdered this morning by Marshall, a maid. His body. . . ."

Webb's eyes blazed at him with a mixture of defiance and fear. "Wot's that you say? By who?" he blurted out.

"By Marshall, I said," rattled back Baddeley. "Would you prefer me to say, by *Mrs. Webb*?"

As the full significance of his statement sank into the "Spider's" mind his face blanched with terror. "She found him . . . murdered . . ." he muttered. "How was he done in?"

"He was strangled," responded his accuser. "Strangled by such a thing as a shoe-lace. A shoe-lace like this." He held it in front of him.

Webb licked his lips. "Let me make a statement, Inspector. You put it down as I give it to yer. This is a facer, and no mistake. But on your life, guvnor, I'm as innocent as a new-born babe."

Baddeley made a sign to Roper. He produced his note-book.

Webb moistened his lips again. "It's like this. You've caught me properly and you've taken the goods off of me. There's no gainsayin' that. But I reckon I know when the tide's runnin' against me, and I figure out that time's now. I got the necklace last night, or you can call it, about two o'clock yesterday morning. How you got on to me I can't tell no more than Adam, but here I am with the bracelets on me. S'elp me God, Inspector, I was away from this place by ten minutes past two, and never set eyes on a livin' soul. I'll take my dyin' oath on that."

"You never met Mr. Prescott at all?" asked Anthony.

"I never met nobody and I've never 'eard of Mr. Prescott."

"How do you account for this shoe-lace being found in your pocket?"

"I can't, guvnor, and that's a fact. I can't even say as 'ow it *is* mine."

"What do you mean?"

"Well, if it's mine, it's laid in that pocket for weeks without me noticin' it."

Baddeley turned to Anthony Bathurst. "I don't think we shall gain much by keeping him any longer. I'll send him down with Roper. Yes?" Anthony nodded. But he was apparently far from happy at the singular twist things had taken. I could very well imagine one or two of his preconceived theories had toppled very sickeningly from their citadels. "Motor him down to the station then, Roper."

"Right, sir!"

"Now for an interesting little experiment," said Baddeley. "Wait here a minute, gentlemen." He slipped from the room.

"I hope he won't be too long," said Sir Charles. "It's very late and I'm dead tired. What's this experiment?"

Before either of us could answer, the Inspector reappeared. In his hand he carried the two brown shoes that we had found on Prescott. He proceeded to insert the lace we had just discovered on Webb in the shoe that wanted it. The length was just right.

"The other lace, gentlemen," he declared. "Look for yourselves."

"You're right, Inspector," said Anthony. "Though I must confess I had doubted it."

"Complicates things, considerably, don't you think? Fairly beats me!"

"No," said Anthony. He put his pipe in his pocket. "I regard this as a most interesting and instructive development."

## CHAPTER XII

## MAJOR HORNBY AND THE VENETIAN DAGGER

THE MONDAY afternoon following the murder found Roper busy in the small and unpretentious building in Considine that served as the Police Station. As he worked he muttered to himself. "Take a Kodak with you on your holidays. I don't think. When I get my holidays I'll take darned good care to leave my photography apparatus at home." He looked at the clock. "Just on three o'clock—the Inspector will be here in a jiffy." He held half a dozen plates to the light—then put them down again on the window-sill. "They'll be just about ready for him."

"Good-afternoon, Mr. Roper."

He turned quickly. "Hallo, Griffiths," he said as a constable entered. "Got back all right then?"

Constable Griffiths grinned. "You've said it. Ran 'em into Lewes Jail about half-past eleven this morning—wasn't half a mob as the van drew up. News spreads, don't it, Mr. Roper? Nice job for a Bank Holiday!"

Roper nodded. "Guess they won't call it a honeymoon, that pair," he reflected. "Still, things aren't at all clear. . . ."

"Which one did the job, do you think?" interrogated Griffiths.

"Which job?"

"Why, the murder, of course. What's the Inspector think?" He went on. "I know he ain't holding 'em yet for that job—I was here when they were charged, but he's a dark horse, he is," he chuckled as at some particularly satisfying reminiscence . . . "I've known him years."

"Well, Griffiths, he hasn't confided in me . . . yet," rejoined Roper, "but if you want my opinion, for what it's worth, we aren't by any means at the end of the case . . . not by a long way."

Griffiths showed signs of agreement, sagely. "I gave Dr. Elliott a hand when they brought the body down to the mortuary," he announced with an obvious sense of importance, "unusual thing you know, Mr. Roper, a bloke strangled and stabbed like this one was—like the pictures," he concluded with evident relish.

"Yes," said Roper. "I can tell you it's given the Inspector plenty to think about."

"More in it than meets the eye, eh?" Griffiths delivered this profound opinion with a prodigious amount of head shaking and brow knitting.

"Shouldn't be surprised—but clear out now—here comes the Governor."

Griffiths adjusted his chin-strap. "Right-O—I'll come and see you later."

"Did I hear you talking, Roper?" said Baddeley, as he entered. "Who was it?" As I am entirely indebted to Baddeley himself for the substance of this chapter, I can say with assurance that he mistook the constable's voice for that of Fitch, Sir Charles Considine's butler, hence this rather peremptory opening question—but he was a man who took very few chances—and his mind at this particular time was casting, as it were, backwards and forwards, to grasp any point that seemed of the slightest significance.

"Constable Griffiths, sir," replied Roper. "He's been to Lewes, as you know, sir, with the two prisoners and just got back. They're pretty quiet, he says," volunteered Roper in addition. "Dazed-like."

"Humph!" grunted Baddeley. "Those photographs ready yet?"

"Just about, sir, I think." Roper went to the window and brought them back. Then extracted them, one by one, from their frames.

Baddeley glanced quickly at the first two or three—those of Prescott's dead body lying as we had found it.

"I want the finger-prints and the photo of those on the Venetian dagger," he said impatiently. "I'm puzzled, Roper, the whole case puzzles me—I want to see if any of the prints we got on those interesting letters of yours correspond with those we originally spotted on the dagger."

"Very good, sir," murmured Roper. "There's a beauty there of the dagger prints"—he handed it over to his superior—"the others won't be very long."

"Thanks! A remarkable case, Roper, don't you think?" He went on without giving his assistant time to reply. "A man murdered in a country house, with two weapons employed—although according to the medical testimony the shoe-lace did the job effectively and the dagger wasn't needed. The body is found in the billiard room on the billiard-table—in evening dress and brown shoes. Where's the motive?"

"Ah, that's it, sir," interposed Roper. "Find that and you'll see daylight."

"Well," went on Baddeley, "there are three people against whom we can lodge a motive or a partial motive." He ticked them off on his fingers. "(One) Webb—Prescott interrupted him or was in some way connected with him . . . he had been out that night on some pretext. (Two) Lieutenant Barker—he had financial reasons for wishing Prescott out of the way—and his I.O.U. cannot be traced. (Three) Major Hornby—he was Barker's friend and brother officer. And had lost money to Prescott similarly. Also he was the reverse of candid when I spoke to him." He paused and considered. "They're the three I've got something against, Roper, and one of those three had the shoe-lace in his pocket. Pretty conclusive, some people would say, and yet . . . and yet. I'm not satisfied. Can you see the unusual features of this affair, Roper?"

"Seem to me a large number, sir," answered Roper. "Do you mean any particular one?"

"I mean this. Everybody in the house has got the same alibi—of course an unsupported and unsatisfactory one, I admit—but there it is. 'I was asleep, Inspector.'"

"I suppose if the murdered man were here and could speak, he'd say he was asleep too!" Roper grinned at the sally.

"Young Mr. Considine and Captain Arkwright admitted to a certain amount of wakefulness, sir," he reminded the Inspector.

"Yes—I know. Arkwright heard the 'Spider'—I've no doubt on that point—Jack Considine may have heard anything—Marshall—Mrs. Webb, if you prefer it—possibly leaving the billiard room—it's an idea certainly."

Roper pursed his lips together. "It's the motives some people *may* have had, sir, the motives that have to be probed for. What's that bit the French say about looking for a woman always?"

"*Cherchez la femme*," said Baddeley. "I wonder."

"Any one of the people up at the Manor may be guilty, sir, it seems to me," continued the indefatigable Roper, "and then again it may come back quite simply and directly to 'Spider' Webb. The job is to pick out the main trail and not go dashing off into side tracks that eventually become blind alleys."

"Very true, Roper, very true," smiled Baddeley. "But it isn't quite so easy as you imagine; one of your side tracks may turn out to be that main trail and what you think is the main trail, may prove to be only a side track."

"That Mr. Bathurst's a smart young fellow, sir. He'd have done well in our line, don't you think so?"

"Perhaps! You can't always tell. What about those prints?"

Roper took them out. "They're all numbered, sir. And I've got the corresponding numbers in my note-book. And I fancy we've got pretty well everybody here. Everybody that's likely, that is!" He paused. Then continued: "We haven't got the 'Spider's,' sir. You haven't forgotten that, have you? . . . And I'm thinking his are the most likely."

"No, I know, Roper. Easily get those from 'the Yard' if necessary."

Roper arranged the photographs. "I'll put them in numerical order, sir, that will simplify matters a bit."

Baddeley picked up his magnifying glass and proceeded on his course of comparison. But one by one he laid the photos down again. Then suddenly he shot up from his seat.

"You've clicked, Roper!" he shouted. He looked at the back. "Number 9," he exclaimed, "number nine for a certainty, look—the identical loops and whorls—who in the name of thunder is Nine—where's your note-book—quick, man, quick!" The prints had come out clearly and distinctly. And when compared with the photograph of those on the Venetian dagger, there didn't remain the shadow of a doubt that the same fingers had made them. Roper flicked the leaves of his note-book. "Number Nine, sir?" he queried. He ran his eye down the page. "Major Hornby!"

Baddeley gasped. "This beats the band, Roper, but all the same, mark my words, one of the three with a motive that's known. Well, I'm blessed."

Roper looked wise and said nothing.

Baddeley's mind went back. "He practically refused all information when I questioned him, and told me to mind my own business. If he's the murderer of Prescott he reckons we've got no proof at all . . . he'll try to put up a big bluff. Now where do I stand? All I can put against him so far is a motive, finger-prints on a dagger that has played some part in the crime . . . anything else? I can't put a truculent manner and attitude in as compromising evidence." He paced the room—backwards and forwards. "Gets a darned sight more complicated every step," he grumbled.

"This dagger was kept in the drawing-room, wasn't it, sir?" said Roper.

"So I'm told. On what they called the curio table. What are you driving at?"

"Well, I don't somehow think the 'Spider' ever got into the drawing-room."

"Marshall may have taken it from the table."

"Why don't her finger-prints show then, sir?"

"True . . . Major Hornby seems to have been the last person to have used it."

"He could easily have taken it to his bedroom, sir," continued Roper.

"Yes, he slept alone. It's feasible. But why the deuce was Prescott outside that night?" Baddeley blazed. "Tell me that and I'll tell you a lot more . . . nothing I light on seems to have any bearing on that point. And till I know, I'm messing round in the dark."

"Where does this Major Hornby hang out, sir?" questioned Roper.

"Don't know at the moment, but Sir Charles Considine will let me know at once if I ask him. I think I will."

Anthony and I were in the garden when the Inspector arrived. He looked worried and puzzled but determined.

"Good-afternoon, gentlemen, Sir Charles about and handy?"

Anthony looked at me. "Yes," I said, "you'll probably find him in the library."

"Thank you." He passed through into the house, and it was not for some days that I learned of the reason underlying his visit or what transpired at his interview with Sir Charles Considine. Our host, I imagine, was not too pleased at Baddeley's reappearance. We had had a brief period of comparative quiet after the arrest of Webb and his wife, and Sir Charles was expecting to be left alone until the inquest. This advent of Baddeley disturbed him and brought back the sinister influences that he had been trying to forget.

"The address of Major Hornby? Of course you can have it! But surely, Inspector, you don't harbour any suspicions against a gentleman of Major Hornby's standing?"

"Not at all, Sir Charles," replied Baddeley cheerfully. "I merely want a little more information from the Major on one particular point than he was able to give me when I saw him previously. That is all, sir."

Sir Charles rummaged through his pigeonholes. "Major Hornby is a man of unimpeachable integrity, Baddeley—a British Officer—don't forget—and—er—a gentleman. Here's the address." He turned a card over. Baddeley took it. "Melville's Hotel, Canterbury," he read.

"Thank you, Sir Charles. Please accept my sincere apologies for disturbing you. By the way—the inquest has been fixed for Thursday."

Sir Charles thanked him, and the Inspector bowed himself out.

"I want you to motor me over to Canterbury, Roper," he announced as soon as he got back. "Major Hornby's staying there—it shouldn't take us too long although, being Bank Holiday, the roads are certain to be pretty thick." A couple of hours' journey took them over, and shortly afterwards the car drew up outside Melville's Hotel.

The Inspector sent up his card with the request that he might see the Manager. A tall man—dark and rather military-looking—quickly attended upon him.

Baddeley told him his errand. "Major Hornby is staying here—certainly—he arrived late on Saturday evening—but he is not in at the present moment."

"Would he be likely to be long?" inquired the Inspector.

The Manager didn't think so—he would speak to one of the waiters. Would the Inspector be kind enough to excuse him for a moment? Baddeley kicked his heels in the vestibule. But his patience was not strained for long. "Major Hornby is expected back for dinner—he has asked his waiter to reserve him a corner seat at one of the dining-tables. Will you wait, Inspector, or call back in about an hour?" Baddeley thought the matter over for a moment and decided to call back.

"Roper," he said as he entered the car, "drive to a nice little pub, where we can get a Guinness and something to eat in a certain amount of seclusion. I'm getting a bit peckish."

Now this was a job near Roper's heart, and he lost little time in the fulfilment of the instruction. The saloon they entered was moderately full, and divided into two compartments, one of which was curtained off and designated, "Smoke Lounge." Baddeley elected to remain in the ordinary compartment and was just settling down to the enjoyment of his "snack" when the fragment of a conversation from the other side of the curtain arrested his attention and screwed all his faculties to their highest pitch. "Well, Barker," said a voice that sounded strangely familiar, "I'm glad I met you as you suggested—and I'm more than glad that you've come to me for advice. I've given it to you, and I hope you'll decide to take it. It's always as well in affairs of this kind, to make a clean breast to somebody. And I don't imagine that the truth will ever be brought to light now—so you can rest in peace."

Baddeley's eyes met Roper's—he put his finger to his lips.

"Thanks awfully, Major," came the reply, "it's been no end of a worry wondering what has been found out, and what hasn't, and I'm deuced glad to have told you. I'll say good-night"; and before Baddeley could offer any further warning—the heavy, dark-blue curtain parted and there stepped out Lieutenant Barker. Without noticing their presence, he strode across the apartment and disappeared. The Inspector gripped the edge of the table with his fingers. Then he leaned across and addressed his companion.

"I'm going to strike while the iron's hot," he whispered. "You stay here and listen—I'm going in there to have a word with Major Hornby. Don't move from this table till you see me again."

Roper accepted the situation with an understanding nod, and Baddeley pushed the curtains to one side and stepped through.

"Good-evening, Major Hornby," he said cordially. "May I sit down?"

Major Hornby looked up in amazement. Then his breeding got the better of his inclinations. He suffered himself to return the Inspector's greeting. He then turned nonchalantly to the table and emptied his glass. This accomplished he rose as though to go. Baddeley raised his hand.

"I want a word with you, Major," he spoke very quietly, and not without dignity, "and, believe me, I have come some miles to get it."

Major Hornby shrugged his shoulders. Then he spoke very coldly. "You are imposing a distinct strain on my forbearance,

Inspector Baddeley—I have already given you all the information I can. That should satisfy even your fund of curiosity."

"All the information you *can*?" queried Baddeley, "or all the information you intend to give me?"

Hornby eyed him with strong disfavour. "Call it what you choose."

Baddeley's impatience mastered him. "Look here, Major," he said, "I'm going to be perfectly frank with you, and I'm not going to beat about the bush." Hornby raised his eyebrows.

"I'm afraid I'm at a loss to—"

Baddeley cut him short. Lowering his voice considerably he leaned right across the table, and something in his persistence compelled Hornby to listen attentively. "You will remember, Major, that Mr. Prescott besides having been strangled—had been stabbed at the base of the neck with a dagger—known to Sir Charles Considine, your late host, and to his intimates, as the Venetian dagger?"

Major Hornby showed signs of assent. The Inspector proceeded. "That dagger was prepared and photographed on my instructions, immediately after I first arrived on the scene, and on the result showed a distinct set of finger-marks." His companion began to show evidence of interest. "Now, Major," and here Baddeley grew grave, "I made it my business to obtain a set of finger-prints of the various people I encountered in the house"—he was studying Hornby very carefully now—"and I have compared the incriminating set with the specimens I managed to obtain." He paused.

"I'm all attention, Inspector," said the Major. "And you discovered—?"

"That the finger-prints were *yours*—Major Hornby."

"Really, Inspector—now that's most interesting—when are you going to arrest me?"

Baddeley waved the sarcasm on one side. "Can you explain what I have just told you?"

Hornby pulled at his top lip, thoughtfully.

"Quite easily to a point," he said. He looked at the Inspector, who showed no sign. Hornby went on. "I held that dagger in my hand on the evening before Prescott was murdered."

"What were the circumstances?"

The Major smiled. "Nothing suspicious. After dinner that evening, we were talking about crime—"

Baddeley was immediately alert. "What? Who was?"

"All of us. The conversation was general. Why do you ask?"

"Who was responsible for the turn the conversation took? Anybody in particular—think carefully—it may be of the greatest importance?"

"Well, if you ask me, Inspector, it was Bathurst—he rather fancies himself, you know, in the sleuth line. Can't think of anybody else. Yes, I'm sure he began it."

Baddeley nodded. "All right! Go on!"

Hornby reflected. "Where was I?"

"Talking about crime," muttered his companion grimly. "Only talking—"

"Oh yes! Well, the conversation got pretty well going—murders and detectives and what not, and it didn't seem likely that cards would be started for some little time—and I wandered round the drawing-room. When I got to the curio table, as it was called, my eyes fell on the Venetian dagger. I couldn't help thinking how it fitted in with the subject of the reigning conversation. I picked it up and examined it with some interest—and the thought came to me that it might have sent more than one soul into eternity."

The Inspector listened eagerly, and with some impatience.

"Yes, yes!" he said. "What then?"

Major Hornby shook his head—"There's nothing more to tell. I put the dagger back on the table and shortly afterwards started to play cards."

Baddeley thought for a moment. His next question the Major thought surprising.

"Tell me, Major Hornby," he said, "when you were examining the dagger, did you by any chance happen to notice if any person in the room was watching you?"

Hornby looked him straight in the eyes. "That's very remarkable—because I did."

"Who was it?" The Inspector's eyes gleamed with excitement.

"Gerald Prescott!"

Baddeley pushed his chair back—then mastered his discomfiture. Hornby eyed him with cool nonchalance. "And I can tell you something else of importance. When I went to bed that night—the Venetian dagger had gone from the curio table!! Because I looked."

## CHAPTER XIII

## MR. BATHURST POTS THE RED

THE NEXT MORNING Mary joined me in the garden—just after breakfast. She looked lovelier than ever, although it was obvious to the careful observer that she was troubled. "Bill," she said, "you haven't spoken to poor Mrs. Prescott since her arrival yesterday—she had all her meals in her room, you know—come and see her this morning—if only to please me. It's been heart-breaking to talk to her. He was her only son."

I was conscious of a certain feeling of resentment. It was absurd of her upsetting herself like this—Prescott was dead and it was all exceedingly sad and all that—but it didn't please me to see the shadows in Mary's face over it. I gently remonstrated with her.

"You mustn't let yourself be worried about this affair, Mary," I said, "it's bad enough I know, and pretty sickening happening here and at this time—rotten for Sir Charles and your mother—but hang it all, it might have been a lot worse."

She looked at me reproachfully. "What do you mean," she asked, "in what way?"

"Well," I responded, awkwardly I admit, "it might have been Jack—or—er Captain Arkwright—one of the family you might say—Prescott wasn't exactly a 'nearest and dearest.'"

She scanned my face curiously. "No, Bill," she remarked very quietly, "he wasn't exactly. But I've had to face his mother and I can't forget that he was our guest and that it was in our house that he met his death—that he came to his death here," she wrung her hands in the emotion of her distress—"it makes me feel so responsible."

"Rot!" I exclaimed, "it might have happened to him anywhere—you can't prevent a crime—now and then."

"It might have, Bill, but it didn't. And that's just all that matters."

"Again, it might have been worse, too, from the other stand-point."

"What do you mean?"

"Your mother's pearls. We've recovered them when the odds seemed pretty hopeless."

"What do they matter? Bill"—she put her hand on my sleeve, "you can do me a favour. Tell Mr. Bathurst I should like to have a chat with him."

"When?"

"Oh—when it's convenient—this afternoon, say."

"All right," I replied. "What are you doing this morning?"

"I'm going to take Mrs. Prescott out of herself—if I can. Come and see her."

I disliked the job as much as Mary had dreaded it, but courtesy demanded it.

Mrs. Prescott was a tall woman with white hair—somewhere I should judge in the early "fifties." She was completely mistress of her feelings and gave an immediate impression of efficiency and capability. I learned afterwards that she had founded the florist's business in Kensington that had achieved such remarkable success and had been the foundation stone of the family fortunes, and was herself at the time of which I speak a Justice of the Peace. The blow she had received had been a very heavy one, but she was unmistakably facing it with courage.

"Good-morning, Mr. Cunningham," she greeted me quietly.

"You know me then, Mrs. Prescott?" I asked, not without surprise.

"Gerald"—there was a little catch in her throat—"pointed you out to me at Lords' a month ago."

I was momentarily at a loss. I had expected a grief-stricken woman bordering on hysteria, and this quiet and courageous resignation stirred me greatly.

"I see," I responded. Then murmured a few words of condolence.

"Thank you," she said, "thank you. As you say, Mr. Cunningham, his death is a terrible thing—but the idea that he has been murdered, and that his memory will be attached for always to that murder, I find even more terrible and nerve-racking. If I don't summon all my strength to my aid—I fear I shall give way to the horror of it."

I expressed my most sincere sympathy, and Mary Considine caught her two hands and pressed them.

"You're wonderful," she cried, "to endure things as you have. And I'm going to try to help you to endure them even better."

Mrs. Prescott smiled very sweetly. "You are very kind, my dear," she said. "But I feel this, Mr. Cunningham," she turned in my direction, "that I owe it to my son's memory to leave no stone unturned to find the man or woman who killed him." The look of patient resignation on her face gave way to one of steady resolution. She continued—talking seemed to relieve her grief a little, perhaps.

"I'm certain of one thing. I'm absolutely certain, in my own mind, that when Gerald came down here to Considine Manor, he had no worries, no trouble on his mind, and that whatever dark passions encompassed his end—were awakened very recently."

Mary's eyes brimmed with tears.

"Oh, don't say that, Mrs. Prescott," she said. "I can't bear to think that this came to him when he was our guest—I've just been telling Mr. Cunningham the same thing."

Mrs. Prescott smiled sadly. "You have nothing with which to reproach yourself, my dear. I just know that when Gerald came here he was intensely happy and glad to come. Therefore, whatever cause brought about his death, had its origin down here.

That's all I mean." She put her arm round Mary's shoulders. I heard a step behind—it was Anthony. Mary introduced him.

"I am pleased to meet Mr. Bathurst," said Mrs. Prescott. "I have heard already from Sir Charles Considine of what you have done for him. Perhaps you will be able to do something for me."

Anthony bowed. "I am at your service, Mrs. Prescott—command me. How can I help you?"

She repeated to him her previous words to us. Anthony knitted his brows.

"I appreciate," he said, "the fact that you are speaking with intimate knowledge which makes what you say especially valuable—you are quite assured that your son had no shadow on his life when he came down here?"

"I am positive of it, Mr. Bathurst," Mrs. Prescott replied. "Of course it may have been some phase of the robbery Mary has told me about, but something tells me it wasn't—the cause lies outside that." She shook her head.

"Pardon me, Mrs. Prescott," interposed Anthony. "I should like to ask you a question—can you in any obscure or roundabout way connect your son—legitimately of course—with any previous jewel robbery?"

A look of amazement spread over her features.

Anthony continued quickly. "I'm afraid I've put it to you very awkwardly and clumsily—but this is what I'm driving at. Has he, for example, ever been stopping at a country house that has been robbed while he has been there? The kind of experience, we will say, that would cause him to be on the *qui vive* were he confronted a second time with the possibility?"

"I don't altogether follow you, Mr. Bathurst," she answered, "so I don't know whether I can answer you satisfactorily—but I don't know of any connection of the kind you have indicated."

"I have a reason for asking," he intervened quickly. "There is abundant circumstantial evidence that your son, on the evening of the murder, may have been outside the billiard room window—almost in the same spot as this man Webb. If it were he, what took him there?"

"If he were there, Mr. Bathurst," said Mrs. Prescott, "you may depend upon it, that he had a good and honourable reason for going."

Anthony bowed. "I see no reason to doubt the accuracy of your opinion."

"Thank you, Mr. Bathurst."

"But, all the same, I must confess to being mystified with regard to those footprints."

"The whole affair is a mystery," she answered, "that may never be solved."

"Not the whole affair, Mrs. Prescott—some aspects are becoming increasingly plain—and I hope in time to solve it all!" Anthony's jaw set.

"That will mean a lot to me, Mr. Bathurst," she said. "Perhaps more than I can tell you." She turned to Mary. "I'll come with you now, dear, as you suggested. Good-bye to you two gentlemen. But there, I'm sure to see you again." They passed out of the room together and left us.

"What are you doing this morning, Holmes?" I sallied. Anthony looked at me whimsically.

"I'm thinking of having another look at things," he said; "there are one or two things I should like to make more sure of."

"What are they?" I inquired curiously.

"I should like to have a look at the billiard room—and Prescott's bedroom," he replied unconcernedly. "I'm building up a theory and I would like to test it in one or two places. Come with me?"

"Delighted," I answered. "Billiard room first?"

"As you please," said he. We ascended the stairs. In the sunshine of the morning, there seemed to remain no trace of the dreadful secret the room held. The table, bereft of its ghastly burden of a few days since, only spoke of the game it stood for. It was a difficult matter to realize all that had happened since the last game that had been played upon it.

"These chairs were overturned, Bill, and this poker was lying on the floor—remember?"

I did—and I said so. He went full length on the floor and took a magnifying-glass from his pocket.

"I'm rather sceptical about the magnifying-glass stunts you get in detective novels," he muttered, "but I want an extra-special look at this floor-covering.

"No," he said as he arose, "I can't see any signs of any struggle—there are no scratches that would evade the naked eye, of feet moved uncontrollably like in a fight or wrestle. And what is more, Bill, I particularly noticed when Marshall gave the alarm, that although Prescott's brown shoes were muddy—there was no trace of any mud on the floor here. Think of that, laddie."

"It might happen so," I ventured.

"Hardly likely, Bill! There was an appreciable amount of mud on the brown shoes, and one would reasonably expect to find a few traces if Prescott had been engaged in a struggle. In a fight or a wrestle—such as might have taken place here, there is far more pressure of the feet on the ground and certainly more friction than is got by ordinary walking—don't you see?"

"Yes," I conceded. "I see what you mean."

"Yet," he went on, "I am certain that there were no mud-marks on the floor. Which suggests a number of entertaining possibilities." He frowned.

"You haven't told me yet," I urged, "of those three definite clues you picked up right at the outset. Still liking the look of them? I'm curious!"

"One of 'em has been dragged to light, Bill, and I'm very satisfied with its results—the other two I'm still keeping—for the time being at all events."

I felt annoyed. All faithful Watsons were not treated in this cavalier manner. They were always admitted willingly and readily into the confidential intimacies. I voiced a complaint. I thought a semi-humorous strain might become the matter best.

"How, my dear Anthony," I began, "can you reasonably expect to be guided by the best gleams of my superlative intelligence and highly-powered imagination, if you persist in withholding important information from me?" He flashed a smile at me. Then his face took on a more serious aspect.

"Pardon me, Bill—not exactly information. You have seen the same things as I have seen—I'm keeping nothing from you—the difference is that a certain two points made a vivid impression on me—and they didn't on you."

"All right, then," I returned, "I plead guilty. What were they?"

"If I tell you, Bill, and eventually we find that their significance was much less than I imagine, you'll never believe in me again—and I can't possibly run the risk of that."

I could see that nothing I could do would shake his determination. So I turned the subject.

"Are you in a hurry to look over Prescott's bedroom again?"

"It depends on what you mean by a 'hurry.'"

"Well, what about a 100 up before we go?" I took a cue and walked to the billiard-table.

"Right-O," said Anthony. "A little relaxation won't harm either of us."

The three balls were in the bottom right-hand pocket where they had lain, presumably, for some days.

"Let's have them," I cried. "Spot or Plain?"

"Anything," he answered. "Spot!" He put his flat hand, palm upwards, underneath the pocket and sent the balls rolling on to the green cloth.

"Go on," I said, "break." He opened by giving me the usual point. I replied by coming off the red ball on to the spot-ball and in attempting a second cannon I failed, leaving the red nicely in front of the bottom right-hand pocket. Anthony smiled in appreciative approval.

"Thank you, Bill!" He promptly potted the red. "I can see visions of a nice healthy little break here," said he, as he sidled round to pick the red ball out. He plunged his hand into the pocket. Then I saw his face register surprise.

"What's up?" I queried half-interestedly.

"Something down here in the pocket, Bill," he returned. "A piece of paper." He drew out a twisted piece of paper and smoothed it out with his fingers—it was a portion of envelope. In a second it flashed into my mind what it was. Something seemed to hammer it into my brain instantaneously. Before my tongue could give sound to the message that was flooding my brain Anthony spoke very quietly, and very gravely. I remember that I marvelled at the time that he could retain so undisturbed an equanimity.

"Bill," he said, "Barker's I.O.U.! By Jove!"

"How the devil did it come there?" I exclaimed.

He thought for a second or two before replying. "Well, taking all the circumstances into consideration, not such an unlikely place, after all, to find it. Prescott's body lay across this table, near this particular pocket, and it's quite conceivable that (1) the I.O.U. fell in some manner from his coat pocket into the billiard-table pocket or (2) the I.O.U. was taken from the body by the murderer, and dropped, either in the struggle or afterwards. The murderer might even have searched the room for it—assuming that he wanted it badly—and never imagined that it had fallen where it had."

"Yes," I assented. "I follow you. How was it"—I went on—"that you didn't notice it when you took the balls out just now?"

"There were three balls in this pocket then. I knocked them out from *outside* the pocket—when I plunged my hand *in* to get out the red ball, I felt this piece of envelope."

"I see."

"And there's something more that I can contribute, Bill!" He wrinkled his forehead as was his habit when endeavouring to remember something very accurately or in extreme detail. "When we were called to this room at seven o'clock that morning by Marshall, the three balls were in the pocket then. I can recall them distinctly—Prescott's body was lying across the bottom of the table. He was partly on his right shoulder, and his right arm was hanging over the side—very near the pocket where I've found the I.O.U. I can remember looking at the limp arm hanging there—and then looking into the pocket and seeing the balls. I can—" he stopped suddenly. "But there's something wrong somewhere, there's a difference—there's a—" he thrust his hands into his pockets and paced the room. When he turned in my direction again, I could see that his eyes were closed. He was thinking hard. "It will come back to me," he muttered.

"There was the arm—there were the three balls—there was the dagger—" he snapped his fingers. Then he swung around.

"Got it?" I asked curiously.

"Got what?"

"Whatever was eluding you?"

He smiled. "I think so," he answered, "anyway the three balls were there—it was impossible to see the piece of envelope even if we had thought of looking there. But, I must confess, it didn't occur to me. And evidently also, it didn't occur to the worthy Baddeley."

"Going to tell him?" I queried.

"Afraid we ought to! Still I don't see why we should . . . yet. On second thoughts, I think we'll put it back in its little nest . . . in this self-same pocket. For the time being, William, we will remember, we twain, that 'Silence is Golden' and that Inspector Baddeley didn't call us a lot of 'tight-lips' unreasonably."

I looked at the I.O.U. There it was as Barker had described it. Just a mere scrawl. But possibly it had cost a man his life. And might cost another his. "I.O.U. £208. Malcolm V. Barker." Anthony held his hand out for it. "Let's put it back, Bill. It will suit my book if it lie there for a time." He tucked it away into the pocket. "Going on with the game?"

I shook my head. "I've lost interest—this new turn has done it. I don't feel anything like so keen."

"Neither do I. What about having another look at Prescott's bedroom? You remember what I told you just now!"

But I was reluctant to turn my thoughts from our latest discovery. I was anxious to hear more of what Anthony thought with regard to it. Had he formed one of his brilliantly definite notions or was he still groping for an elusive factor and groping unsuccessfully? I determined to draw a bow at a venture. I might, by so doing, discover something of what lay in his mind.

"I'm afraid," I ventured with an air of wisdom, "that this latest business brings the searchlight of suspicion on to Lieutenant Barker again—don't you agree?" I looked at him intently, trying to read his thoughts.

"Why—particularly?"

"Doesn't it make it appear," I asked, "that Prescott was murdered for possession of that I.O.U.? £200 odd is a pretty substantial sum, you know, for a young officer to lose at a sitting. At least, I'd think so."

"It's a possibility," came the reply, "but you can't assert that the I.O.U. was a primary factor in the murder. I know that the I.O.U. has been discovered near the body, but after all, the explanation may be perfectly simple. Prescott, we will argue, taking the simple line that I have indicated, took the I.O.U. from Barker at the card-table, as we have been told, placed it in the breast-pocket of his dress-coat, and in the struggle that took place when he was done to death, the thing dropped from its place into the pocket of the billiard-table. I told you so just now."

"Certainly a possibility," I said, "but—"

"You don't think so, eh?"

"Well, candidly," I rejoined, "I'm not convinced."

"Nor am I." He smiled again. "I'm only discussing possibilities. Still"—he proceeded more slowly, "I'm inclined to think that this discovery tends to eliminate Barker from our list of suspects."

"Can't see it—quite," I intervened. "I think it's rather damaging to him."

He looked at me keenly.

"I think this," he said. "If Lieutenant Barker had been after that I.O.U.—sufficiently enthusiastic for its possession to murder a man—that once he had got his claws on it, he would have destroyed it."

"How?" I said—"and where? He was bound to keep it for a time—he couldn't destroy it directly he got it—he might have left traces—that would have inevitably incriminated him!" I was jubilant—I felt I had scored.

Anthony lit a cigarette. "Bill," he conceded, "you're right— that's certainly a point that I had not considered!"

# Chapter XIV
# MARY CONSULTS MR. BATHURST

THERE WAS a tap at the door. "May I come in?" It was Mary Considine's voice. I remembered what she had asked me in the garden that morning. "I hope I'm not intruding," she spoke in unusually low tones, "or not interrupting any important conference. Am I? Be sure and tell me if I am."

"Not at all," responded Anthony. "Why do you ask?"

"Because I wanted a little consultation with you, Mr. Bathurst—didn't Bill tell you—I asked him to tell you this morning? Did you forget, Bill?"

I pleaded guilty with apologies to both my companions.

"I am entirely at your service," exclaimed Anthony. "Where would you like this little chat to take place? Here? Or elsewhere?"

"Here will be as convenient to me as anywhere, Mr. Bathurst—that is if you have no objection?"

"I?" He laughingly disclaimed any such idea. "None at all. Now, what have you got to tell me?"

Mary shot him a swift glance from under those long-lashed lids of hers. "What makes you think I have anything to tell you, Mr. Bathurst?" she asked.

He smiled one of his irresistibly-attractive smiles. "I think it's a fairly safe conclusion to which to come. You want a consultation with me. You would hardly put it in that way if you required any information from me—would you—therefore, I imagine you have something to tell me. Am I wrong?"

She flung herself on to the edge of the billiard-table and sat there—dainty and well-shod. She was always as fit as a fiddle and better at games than a good many men. She played a smashing good game of tennis, was a steady bat and bowled quite a good ball—slow, with a deceptive flight that did a little bit both ways—was a good hand with a golf-club, and could make a hundred on the billiard-table in double quick time. As I've said before in this history—Mary Considine was a peach.

"No, you are not wrong, Mr. Bathurst. You are right, of course—but now that I've decided to tell it to you, and have arrived at the moment of the telling—I don't know whether I should or whether it's of the slightest importance—except to me—and—one other."

She stopped and Anthony waited for her to continue.

It was plain to me, interested auditor that I was, that Mary was waiting for some sign of encouragement or approbation from Anthony—but it did not come. She glanced at him, but his eyes were inscrutable.

"You don't help me much," she said, rather deliciously. "You could—you know!"

"I would much prefer you to tell your story entirely in your own way. It is impossible for me, at this stage of the conversation, to judge whether it will possess any significance—please proceed."

She looked rather aggrieved at this, and I wondered what was coming next.

"I haven't told my father. I haven't told my mother—the only person that knows is my sister, Helen—Mrs. Arkwright, you know—I told her soon after it happened. I have had a talk with her over it, Mr. Bathurst, and she approves of my telling you." She clasped her hands. "'Nil nisi bonum de mortuis est,' they say, don't they, and although I'm not going to say anything at all bad—I feel that I'm betraying a confidence—exposing to the world something that he would have regarded as intimate and private—that's why I hesitated and seemed to be in a difficulty just now." She looked at Anthony earnestly, as though probing his mind for his opinion on the matter.

"I appreciate your diffidence, Miss Considine, and I think I can gauge exactly what your feelings are."

She smiled with gratification. "Do you know, that's very nice of you . . . that will make it easier for me to know that. What I want to tell you is this—Gerald Prescott was in love with me and had asked me to be his wife."

I gasped! Consummate effrontery I called it, even though the man was lying dead now.

Anthony appeared to take the news very quietly.

"When did he ask you that?" he queried.

"During the luncheon interval of Friday—the last day's cricket we had."

"I don't wish to appear inquisitive, and believe me I am not asking idly or frivolously—what was your reply?"

Mary blushed a little and her eyes fluttered in my direction.

"I will tell you, Mr. Bathurst, I told him that I would give him his answer the next day—that was all I told him."

"I am going a little further then—what was your answer going to be?"

She looked at me again, then shook her head.

"I don't know, Mr. Bathurst. To be perfectly frank with you, I don't really know—he was too good an athlete to take chances with."

Anthony raised his eyes with an expression of bewilderment. "Too good an athlete? I don't quite understand."

Mary blushed again—then appealed to me to help her out.

"I forgot for the moment that you haven't been here lately, Mr. Bathurst—tell him for me, Bill—will you, please?"

"Mary swore a fearful oath a few years ago," I explained, "that she would marry no man that couldn't beat her at cricket—single wicket and also over eighteen holes at golf—so that if she goes so far in the matter as to play the two matches it's a kind of half acceptance of his proposal. For if she loses the two games—she pays forfeit. See? Neat plan, I say."

Anthony grinned. "And Prescott was too good a man with whom to take liberties—eh?"

"I wasn't sure," she said, blushing furiously. "I wanted time to think."

Anthony paced the room with swift steps. He came to her again. "This proposal was made, you say, the day preceding the murder?"

"Yes! To be exact, about twelve hours before."

"You say your sister, Mrs. Arkwright, was in your confidence regarding Mr. Prescott's proposal. When did you confide in her?"

Mary looked at him—surprised. "To-day," she answered. "Not before!"

"So that not a soul knew of it before Prescott's death?"

"They couldn't have, Mr. Bathurst!" She spoke with conviction.

"Unless—pardon me making the suggestion—unless Prescott himself spoke of it to somebody."

"That's hardly likely, do you think?" she commented, the violet eyes brimming with tears at the recollection of this man who had loved her, and died so tragically in her home, "so improbable that surely we may dismiss the idea?"

"Had Prescott any particular chum in the house-party?"

"I don't think so," she responded. "Bill might know better than I."

"Had he, Bill?" Anthony fired the question at me.

"No! I should say not. At any rate I hadn't noticed any particular 'Fidus Achates.'"

"I agree with you then, Miss Considine," broke in Anthony. "It is extremely unlikely that he would have confided in anybody."

Then she amazed him with her next remark.

"You don't ask if he had an enemy?"

"What d'you mean?" he said very quietly.

"I mean just this, Mr. Bathurst. I knew very, very little of Gerald Prescott—I had only seen him two or three times before this Cricket Week commenced. And I am positive that during the past week—somebody has been trailing him—spying on him would be the better term."

I felt myself growing excited. We seemed to go from unexpected to unexpected as we progressed in this affair. What was she going to tell us now?

"I take it you have a definite reason for saying this, Miss Considine?" asked Anthony gravely. "What are your facts?"

"I have, Mr. Bathurst, and when you have heard what I am going to tell you, I think you will agree with me. The first time I noticed it was on the Tuesday. After dinner that evening, Gerald Prescott and I walked out into the garden. We came out of the French doors and walked round by the lawn tennis courts. It was a lovely night, and he asked me to sit on the seat at the back of the courts. After we had been sitting there for a little time, I had that peculiar sensation that comes to one, when one is being watched. There are two big trees a few yards away from that seat—at the side of the path that leads to 'The Meadow' and then to the Allingham Road. I turned quickly and looked. There was a man there watching us. He was crouching down and I am almost certain had a soft hat pulled down over his face. . . ." She paused and looked at Anthony.

"This is most interesting, Miss Considine—please go on!"

"I did not tell Mr. Prescott what I had seen, but suggested that we should walk back."

"Would you pass close to the trees on your way back to the house?"

"No. We came up from the corner of the courts and would have the trees on our right."

"At what distance?"

"About twenty yards away. Still, I could see quite clearly—the figure had disappeared."

"Could you give any description of him at all?"

She pondered for a moment. "He seemed to be dressed in darkish clothes—that's all I can say that I could rely upon."

"Physically—how would you place him?"

Here she shook her head. "He was crouched down—his body wasn't in a normal position. I couldn't place him accurately."

"Go on, Miss Considine, tell me of the other times."

"There were two other occasions, Mr. Bathurst. One, the Thursday evening Mr. Prescott and I were again in the garden—it was before the Bridge party started. I purposely walked in the opposite direction to that we had taken on the Tuesday. We came round by the other path—leading past the billiard room and thence to the front of the house. When we reached there, we didn't dally but turned quickly—we were afraid we should keep the card party waiting—and I am certain that we had been followed; I saw a figure crouching against the wall by the turn of the house—sheltering in its shadow. When we turned the figure dodged back quickly—and although we walked back quickly, I never saw it again."

"Did Prescott see it?" queried Anthony.

"He said he didn't when I mentioned it to him, but I am not sure that he wasn't disclaiming the idea in order to stifle any fears I might have had."

"In your opinion, Miss Considine, was it the same man that you had seen on the Tuesday?"

"I couldn't possibly answer that, Mr. Bathurst. Much as I should like to. On this second occasion all I was able to catch sight of was part of a man's body flattened against the angle of a wall."

"I appreciate your difficulty. Now tell me of the third occasion."

"The third time was, comparatively speaking, a trivial incident. On Friday evening—once again, not long after dinner, I was standing with Gerald in the opening of the drawing-room doors leading on to the garden. We were standing just inside the drawing-room. The others were still discussing that 'detective' conversation you yourself had started—Gerald Prescott and I had drifted away. In the midst of our conversation I thought I caught the sound of a very low cough coming from somewhere near—in the garden. When Gerald went in to play cards, I had the temerity to go out there. There was a dark patch of shadow just to the right, by the wall again—and Mr. Bathurst"—she paused dramatically—"all around that patch hung the pungent aroma of a recently smoked cigar." She leaned over and put her hand on his sleeve. "Have I impressed you that some person or persons—was spying on him?"

"What was the conversation between you and Prescott on this last occasion?"

"He was pressing me for a reply to his proposal. The conversation didn't last five minutes."

Anthony looked perturbed. Some element in this latest information was worrying him.

"You didn't give him one, of course, or any indication of your feelings?"

"None. I evaded the issue. We didn't exchange more than half a dozen sentences."

"Tell me, Miss Considine," Anthony became very insistent, "did Prescott, as far as you were able to observe, betray any agitation or emotion, on any one of these three occasions?"

"As far as I was able to judge, Mr. Bathurst, none at all. I am not really sure that he ever saw or heard what I did. If he did, I could not detect that he showed it."

"Thank you. You have told us very plainly and very illuminatingly of what happened. I am very grateful for the information."

"I feel relieved now that I've told you this—it may mean more to you than it has done to me. It may even help you to read this riddle. Frankly, I can't make it out. It would seem to me that Gerald Prescott brought something with him to Considine Manor, something dark and sinister that caused him to be shadowed and spied upon, yet his mother, who should know him best of all, is emphatic that whatever came to him, had its birth and origin here in Considine. Both of us can't be right."

She turned to go. Anthony opened the billiard room door for her, then, as she made her exit, came back to me. I looked at him interrogatively.

"Well?" I asked.

"Well, what, Bill?"

"What next? This is rather a facer, isn't it?"

"A surprising development. You had been here nearly a week, Bill, before I arrived—had you noticed anything of this admiration of Prescott's for Mary Considine?"

"Can't say that I had," I replied after a little reflection—"of course I saw him talking to her sometimes—naturally—but I didn't regard it as a frightfully serious business. Let me put it like this, I fancied that he found her attractive—come to that who wouldn't—but I didn't realize that he was so absolutely bowled over as Mary says."

Anthony took out his cigarette case, selected a cigarette and tapped it carefully.

"This seat by the tennis courts—do you know exactly where she means?"

"Oh yes. Know it well. Why?"

"Well, before we go and have that look at Prescott's bedroom that I spoke about, I think I should like to take a glance at this seat."

"Right-O," I responded. "I'll pilot you there."

We made our way down the garden, turned off to the left, and struck out for the tennis courts.

The trees that Mary had spoken about lay to our left between us and the road to Allingham.

"There's the seat," I said. "We're approaching it the way that Mary says she and Prescott came back. The trees were then, you will remember, on their right." I pointed.

"Quite correct, Bill," came his reply. "According to her version of what happened, the watcher had disappeared when they passed the trees on the journey back. Where did he get to?"

"Probably back into the road," I ventured. "Where he had, doubtless, come from."

"You think so?" he answered. "Let's go and have a look. Come over to the trees themselves." We made our way over. Anthony looked at the seat we had just left, and then turned and gazed across the field to where the Allingham Road lay like a white ribbon across the stretch of Downs.

"What's this shed for?" he inquired. He indicated a wooden building on the opposite side of the path between us and the house.

"It's used for storing the lawn tennis gear," I answered. "Sir Charles Considine had it built near the courts for that purpose."

"Jolly useful place—don't you think, Bill? Very useful indeed."

"Yes," I replied. "Quite a natural idea, though, surely."

"Oh, eminently. But come on—let's be getting back. I've seen all that I want to see."

"Are you going to have a look at the other place where Mary thinks she saw this mysterious watcher—at the angle of the wall past the billiard room window? Or don't you consider it sufficiently important?"

He seemed to have relapsed into a reverie. "Eh—what's that—the other place? No—I don't think I want to see that." He continued. "If I could do what I hinted at in the first place, Bill—sort the actual clues from the false—the whole thing would resolve itself into a plain and simple explanation. There is some evidence that is either merely fortuitous or has been put into the affair with deliberate intent."

He stopped and regarded me very seriously. Then he spoke.

"Bill, I'm inclined to think I'm crossing swords with a very clever criminal, but at the same time, I'm also inclined to think that his cleverness will be his undoing." He rubbed his hands with a kind of pleasurable anticipation.

"Hallo—there's Baddeley! Any more news, I wonder?"

"Good-day, Mr. Bathurst. Good-day, Mr. Cunningham."

"Good-day, Inspector." Anthony eyed him carefully. "You look a wee bit pleased with yourself, Inspector," he sallied.

Baddeley smiled. "You aren't looking too downcast yourself, Mr. Bathurst. All the same I haven't exactly been wasting my time since I had the pleasure of last seeing you."

"Good," replied Anthony. "Going to take me into your confidence at last?"

The Inspector remained silent.

"No? Very unsporting of you—" Anthony grinned. "When are you making your arrest?"

But Baddeley didn't take too kindly to his raillery. "At the right time, Mr. Bathurst, neither before nor after."

Anthony purposely overlooked the acerbity in his tone and continued gaily:

"I'm sure of that, Inspector," then provocatively again— "What I'm afraid of is that you'll collar the wrong person. And my regard for you is such that I'm anxious that you shouldn't."

"I'm not denying it's a very puzzling case, Mr. Bathurst," rejoined Baddeley, "neither am I pretending that it's all as clear as daylight to me—yet—but I'm getting on very nicely, thank you, and the last little ray of sunshine may come at any moment. They very often come when least expected."

Sir Charles Considine, Lady Considine and Jack joined us.

"Ah, Baddeley!" cried Sir Charles—"what luck in your chase—did you get into touch with him all right? Did you get what you wanted?"

"Yes, thank you, Sir Charles—I found him where you said."

"And you were entirely satisfied, eh, Baddeley?"

Baddeley turned the question aside. It didn't suit him at the moment to satisfy Sir Charles' curiosity. "I'll see you later, Sir Charles," he answered, "if you don't mind."

"Oh—quite—quite—I understand perfectly."

"One question I should like to ask you, Sir Charles. On my way here, I met a telegraph boy obviously coming away from the house. Anything important happened since I was here last?"

Sir Charles stared at him blankly. "A telegram here—I wasn't aware—"

Jack Considine cut in. "It was for me, Dad," he said. "From Tennant."

"Tennant?" muttered Baddeley. "Wasn't he a guest here on the night of the murder? What did he want?"

Jack Considine smiled sweetly.

"His pyjamas! He'd left them behind in his bedroom."

## CHAPTER XV

# MR. BATHURST TAKES HIS SECOND LOOK—WITH MR. CUNNINGHAM'S ASSISTANCE

ANTHONY drew me to one side. "I don't think we gain a lot by staying here, Bill," he whispered. "We'll get back to my original proposition—let's have another look at Prescott's bedroom."

We entered the house and went upstairs. It will be remembered that the bedroom occupied by Prescott was the fourth along the corridor, and lay between the rooms that had sheltered Major Hornby and Tennant. It had been straightened and put in order.

Anthony went to the wardrobe and opened it. "Clothes all gone," he remarked.

"Wouldn't the Inspector have them?" I suggested.

"I don't mean the clothes he was wearing—I wanted his other clothes."

"Mrs. Prescott, I expect—that's the explanation. She's taken them."

"Very probably, Bill! Never mind—can't be helped. I daresay she'll let me have a glance at them if I consider it necessary. Let's have a look at the dressing-table drawers. Are they empty too?"

I tried the first—empty. The others were in similar condition—everything had been removed—either by Baddeley or for Mrs. Prescott.

"We're late, old man," I said. "There's nothing here."

Anthony came and looked. "Pity! Still—it's my own fault—I ought to have anticipated this. Delays are dangerous."

He crossed to the window, and looked out, leaving the bathroom door open behind him.

"Precious little chance of any exit or entrance this way," he said. "A cat would find a foothold difficult."

"Why?" I asked. "You didn't really consider that as a possibility, did you?"

"I consider everything as a possibility, Bill—till I know it's not. Hallo—that's rather interesting." He pointed to the washhand basin.

"What is it?" I said.

"The stub of a cigar! Not finished either. Funny place for a cigar."

"Not altogether," I ventured. "Suppose Prescott was smoking a cigar when he came to bed that night and came in here to wash his hands. It would be a very natural thing for him to put it there while he washed them."

Anthony nodded approvingly. "Yes! And when he'd finished washing them?"

"Well?"

"What then? Don't you think he would pick it up again and finish his smoke rather than leave it lying there?"

"Possibly," I responded.

"Rather strange it hasn't been removed," he reflected. "Haven't any servants been here since the murder?"

"Perhaps they did the bedroom and didn't trouble to come in here."

He picked up the portion of cigar. As he had remarked it had certainly not been smoked to the point of necessary relinquishment.

"Remember what Mary Considine told us, Bill? Not long ago?"

"How do you mean?" I said.

"On the third occasion that she fancied Prescott was being watched or followed she went into the garden where she imagined the watcher to be, and detected the smell of cigar smoke. Nothing like conclusive, I know—but certainly pointing in the same direction."

"What brand is it?" I asked.

Anthony demurred. "I am well aware that the immortal Holmes had published a brochure on the various kinds of tobacco ash—I really forget the number he mentioned—but alas! I am unable to keep pace with him there. It looks an ordinary type—I can tell you one thing—it isn't one of Sir Charles Considine's assortment—I've had too many not to know that. Still I'll hang onto it." He put it carefully away in his pocket.

"You'll find that's Prescott's all right," I exclaimed. "How can you imagine it could belong to anybody else? How could anybody else get in here—for a start? In the bathroom of Prescott's bedroom!"

"There's a door, Bill," rejoined Anthony drily. "Quite a natural method of entering a room. You may be quite right, and it may have been Prescott's—all the same I'm going to have a look round in here—there may be more in Mary's story than either of us anticipated." Out came the magnifying-glass again and he got to work with it on the floor of the bathroom.

I strolled back into the bedroom, and couldn't altogether resist a smile as I heard him talking to himself from the farther apartment.

"These criminologists take things extraordinarily seriously," I thought to myself. "Good job if they don't run across too many cases in a lifetime."

I looked round the bedroom. Why shouldn't I try my hand at the sleuth game? Perhaps I could find something! To the best part of my memory Prescott's bedroom had not received too meticulous an examination. After all he had slept and dressed in here for nearly a week, and a bedroom might very easily contain something of his secret, assuming that he possessed one. It was an intimate room—it touched a man—closely. If he had anything to conceal, it might well be that it was hidden in here, somewhere. I wandered round, my eyes searching for likely hiding-places. Inspiration came from nowhere. My eyes caught the bed. Had anybody looked underneath? At any rate I decided that I would! I went down full length and wriggled my body underneath. And I had not been under there many seconds when I formed the opinion that while the floor had nothing to tell me, the wainscoting directly below the head of the bed had three tiny pieces of paper on it! They had fluttered down as very small fragments of paper will, and come to rest on the skirting-board, before reaching the floor itself. Very probably of no consequence whatever, but I'd have old Anthony in, come what may!

I went to the connecting door. "Come in here a minute, will you?"

To all appearances he was engaged in a close scrutiny of the bath-mat. "What's up?" he queried.

I was as near excitement as I had been since this bewildering affair had started.

I beckoned him. "Come in here!" I said. He came with alacrity. I lay at full length as I had done just previously. "Flop down here." He joined me. I pointed to the skirting-board. "See anything there?"

"Only too true," he muttered. "Wonder what it can be! Wriggle up and get it, Bill, the honours are yours, it's your discovery."

I wasted no time to do his bidding.

There were three tiny pieces of paper, just as I had thought. I took them carefully from the little ledge on which they were resting, and crawled out triumphantly from under the bed.

"Good man!" he grinned. "What are they—exactly—now you've fished 'em out? Pieces of a last week's hotel-bill or an announcement of the local flower-show?"

I shook my head. "Remains of a letter," I grunted—"there's handwriting here."

I handed the fragments to him. He took them eagerly. They were obviously small parts of a letter that had been carelessly torn up by somebody in the room, and in the throwing-away process had by some freak of wind or whimsicality, fluttered to the skirting-board. So I reasoned. Anthony spread them out.

I reproduce the three pieces here as nearly as I can remember them after so long an interval.

> I will meet    you in the B    so
> when you                    Mary.
>           at 1.

I gasped! "Good Lord!" I exclaimed. Anthony raised his eyebrows.

"What's this?" he interrogated. "An assignation? Mary?"

"It's Mary Considine," I answered. "It's her handwriting—I've seen it too frequently not to know it. Has she written that to Prescott?"

"No evidence as to whom it's addressed, Bill. We can only conjecture as to that. Also we can only surmise what the capital 'B' stands for."

"What do you think yourself?" I whispered almost fearfully.

"Billiard room, possibly! On the other hand—"

"If it was her way of answering his proposal—why wasn't she frank with us about it? Did she meet him or merely intend to?"

"Look at the handwriting again, Bill! Look at it closely."

I did as he told me. "You're absolutely *certain* it's Mary Considine's writing?" he urged with intensity in his tone. "You haven't the shred of a doubt?"

"Not a shred," I replied. "Not the vestige of a doubt."

"Very well! I'll see her! I'm pretty accurate at summing people up psychologically, and I'm fully prepared for an adequate explanation."

"I'm relieved to hear you say that," I said. "Somehow it goes against the grain to have Mary implicated in this business, even though remotely."

"How came you to look under there, Bill?" he asked suddenly.

"I think I was fired by your example," I replied after a slight pause. "Yes, it was," I went on. "Seeing you poking about in the bathroom started a train of thought in my mind and I decided to have a nose round in here. I glanced at several things in the room, and then suddenly thought of looking under the bed."

He showed signs of approval. "It only shows you that second thoughts often prove to be very valuable. Our decision to take another glance at the billiard room and at this bedroom has brought us a great deal of really important information. We've progressed."

"Do you think so?" I queried rather gloomily, I'm afraid. "It seems to me we're getting deeper and deeper into a kind of morass of doubt and suspicion. Each clue we pick up seems to complicate matters, and contradict the previous one." I sat on the bed. I really meant all that I said. As far as these discoveries went we seemed to be traveling away from a solution and not towards one.

"Be of good cheer, William," cried Anthony jocularly. "All will yet be well."

"I don't know that I share your optimism," I responded—"what's the next move?"

"I'm going to take a rather bold step," he replied. He came and sat himself on the bed beside me. "I'm going to have another word or two with Mary." Then he stretched his long legs out and thrust his hands deep in his trousers-pockets. "Maybe I'm running a certain risk, but in life you have to take risks—I'll take one now." He jumped to his feet—"Coming, Bill?" I found myself wondering what was coming next as we descended the stairs. Where were we going? I loathed the proximity of Mary to the affair at the first onset and this latest development might mean anything.

"Would you be good enough to give me a moment in the library?" asked Anthony when we found her. "Just as a 'quid pro quo'? I gave you a few moments in the billiard room, and now I'm asking you to return the compliment." He smiled and Mary smiled back.

"Of course, Mr. Bathurst! I'll come now! Is it anything important?" she asked when we were settled.

"That's a difficult question to answer, Miss Considine," said Anthony seriously, and with an obviously deliberate choice of words. "You were pleased a short while ago to tell me certain intimate details affecting Prescott and yourself—I appreciated intensely the confidence you imposed in me—you see you've known me for a considerably less time than you have Bill, here." He paused.

Mary intervened. "I don't quite know to where all this is leading—but possibly I share, to a very humble extent, your own gift of character-reading."

Anthony bowed to her. "Thank you—again! I am yielding to the promptings of that gift when I approach you now! And the information that you gave me earlier makes that approach a matter of necessity." He held the three scraps of paper out to her.

"Miss Considine—will you look at these very closely? Is the handwriting yours?"

Mary glanced at the fragments with growing astonishment.

"What is this—please?" she queried.

"Can you help by answering my question first?"

I watched her and saw the amazement in her eyes.

"Very well then—Mr. Bathurst—yes. But I can't—"

"You are certain? I want to be unmistakably certain—certain for instance that it isn't an imitation—a wonderfully accurate imitation?"

She wrinkled her brows and pored over the pieces. When she raised her eyes she betrayed greater wonderment than ever.

"Mr. Bathurst—Bill—I'm absolutely bewildered. I'm certain—positive—as positive as I ever could be about anything—that this is my handwriting—yet I can't recognize the letter from where they've come—I can't even think whom it's to—and if I didn't know that it *was* my handwriting—*I should swear that I hadn't written it*!!"

"You mean," suggested Anthony, "that you don't—"

"I mean this—absurd though it may seem and sound—that I recognize the handwriting, but I don't recognize the *letter*. It is entirely unfamiliar. It appears to me at the moment that I've never previously seen it." The colour flamed in her cheeks and her eyes were bright with excitement. Anthony waited for her to proceed. He seemed to divine what her next question was going to be.

"Tell me," her lips were working tremulously, "what is this? How did it come into your possession?"

"Those three fragments in your handwriting, Miss Considine, were found under the bed in the room recently occupied by Gerald Prescott."

"What?" she exclaimed—indignation challenging surprise in her tone—"Mr. Bathurst—it can't possibly be—I've never written a line to Mr. Prescott in my life."

"Yet they were discovered as I have just said." He spoke very quietly.

"There is some mistake—some mystery," she reiterated.

"Some enemy hath done this—eh?" remarked Anthony.

"I'm dumbfounded—I don't know what to say or suggest. I can't think!"

"Tell me," he said, "I realize the fragments are small, and therefore, not too easy to identify—but there's this point. Do you recognize the notepaper as notepaper that you yourself would have been likely to use?"

She looked at it closely and ran her fingers over its surface.

"Yes," she answered. "It is Considine Manor notepaper—I am sure of that. We have used it for years. I can show it to you."

She went across to Sir Charles Considine's desk that stood in the corner. "Here is some," she said. "Compare it for yourself."

Anthony took it and inspected its texture and quality. Then passed it over to me. There was no doubt about it.

The fragments that I had picked up were pieces of the Manor notepaper.

Then I took a hand. "If you don't recognize the letter, Mary, that these fragments are part of—well, it seems to me that you can't have written it. Don't you see what I mean?"

She gazed at me blankly. Then her reason appeared to reassert itself. "That's just how it appears to me, Bill! That's what I've been trying to tell both of you." She crossed and seated herself again.

"Yet it is your handwriting—you are certain," interposed Anthony.

"Yet it is my handwriting—" she echoed his words in acquiescence.

"It's a staggerer," I exclaimed. "It all seems so completely contradictory."

"The most paradoxical and seemingly contradictory things have sometimes the simplest solutions," remarked Anthony—"when you can find them."

Mary pressed her hands to her brow. "If I could only think clearly about it," she cried wearily, "I'm sure the explanation would come to me—but I can't! I can only repeat what I've previously said—I'm certain it's my handwriting—yet I have no knowledge of the writing beyond that fact." She turned to Anthony. "You say you found the pieces under the bed? Am I to understand you suspected their existence and were looking for them?"

"Bill was the discoverer, Miss Considine—not I," replied Anthony. "I haven't really heard the source of his inspiration."

"It seemed to me there was just a possibility of picking something up in the bedroom"—I tried to bear my blushing honours with modesty—"so I just had a crawl round. Of course it was a piece of terrific luck. A positive thousand to one shot." I looked at Anthony. He had relapsed into a chair—thinking hard. His silence seemed to infect the whole room, and Mary and I sat and regarded each other solemnly. Then Anthony astounded us both. I always knew that his mind had the habit of flying off at surprising tangents, and I was a little prepared for the sudden turn it took now.

"How many cars have you in the garage, Miss Considine?" he asked.

She wrinkled up her forehead in surprise.

"Of our own, do you mean, or including everybody's? I don't quite follow—"

He regarded her steadily.

"Of your own—belonging to Considine Manor, if you prefer it put that way."

"Two."

"What are they?"

"What make—do you mean?"

"Exactly," he answered.

"A 'Daimler' and a 'Morris-Oxford.'"

Anthony made a gesture of annoyance. "Had them long?"

"The Daimler about four years—the Morris-Oxford only a few months—February, I think we bought it. Why?"

He waved her question on one side, swinging a question back to her—"What made you buy it?"

She thought hard for a moment. Then her face cleared. "The other car we had at that time kept giving trouble. The engine was continually giving us trouble."

Anthony leaned across—nervously eager with excitement—"What was the other car—Miss Considine?"

"The old one?—a 'Bean,' Mr. Bathurst."

## Chapter XVI
## THE INQUEST

THE MORNING of the inquest broke beautifully fine and sunny. I looked out of my bedroom window and felt that the duty that lay ahead of us meant putting such a glorious day to poor use. The inquest was to be held at the "Swan's Nest"—the most pretentious hostelry that Considine boasted. I shaved, washed and dressed with an ill grace that morning, for I could remember attending an inquest before—it had bored me beyond expression.

Sir Charles opened the matter at breakfast. "Baddeley tells me they are bringing Marshall in from Lewes for to-day's affair. I was, I confess, somewhat surprised at the news—I had scarcely anticipated such a step. I suppose they know their own business best."

"Who is the coroner for this district, Sir Charles?" asked Anthony.

"A Dr. Anselm. I've had the pleasure of meeting him once or twice before . . . being a magistrate," replied our host.

"It wouldn't astonish me to see a verdict of 'Wilful murder' against 'Spider' Webb," said Jack Considine—"despite what he and this pretty wife of his say about it. What's your opinion, Bathurst?"

Anthony walked across to the sideboard and helped himself to a healthy portion of cold pie.

"Depends entirely upon what Baddeley wants," he responded. "If he's keen on that particular verdict he'll probably play his cards to get it. Personally, I'm not so sure that he is." He went back to the table.

"What makes you think that, Bathurst?" asked Captain Arkwright.

"Oh—I'm not suggesting anything against Baddeley, in any shape or form—but the police have advantages in these matters—they're playing on their own ground as it were." He laughed. "I'm assured in my own mind that it is so—I've watched events pretty closely and often noticed it—still, this Inspector has impressed me throughout as an upright, honest and quite efficient person so we can't tell." He walked back to his seat. Then continued, "And of course, there's always the possibility that he may have something up his sleeve. Personally—I shall expect it."

"Well, Baddeley isn't the only one to have that," I ventured blazingly indiscreet.

Anthony shook a warning finger at me. "Bill—Bill—" The breakfast company immediately became all attention.

"What's this, Bill?" demanded Sir Charles. "Who among us has any special knowledge? Bathurst hasn't made any other discoveries, has he?"

Anthony flung another warning glance in my direction then replied to Sir Charles. "You flatter me, Sir Charles," he said laughingly, "and you make altogether too much of my Webb escapade—Bill is getting as bad as the rest of you—that's all there is to it."

I thought that Sir Charles looked somewhat relieved. Lady Considine evidently had a similar impression for she leaned across and patted him on the sleeve. "Don't you worry too much about it, Charles," she said quietly; "let's get this unpleasant business over to-day—then perhaps we may be allowed to forget. If Inspector Baddeley arrests the murderer—well and good—if he fails to—" she shrugged her shoulders. The breakfast party broke up.

"Both the cars are going down to the village—there will be room in them for all," announced our host.

We murmured our thanks. "What do you say to a stroll down, Bill?" said Anthony. "Plenty of time, and it will stretch our legs."

"I'm with you," I responded. I was secretly pleased at the opportunity—I imagined that he wanted to tell me something or desired to discuss some aspect of the case with me. I was disappointed. He was quiet. We swung along some distance before I broke the ice.

"What did you make of that letter business?" I asked, watching his expression intently.

"In what relation?"

"To Prescott—to the murder." I was nettled. What relation did he imagine I meant?

"Oh, that! None at all!"

I stared incredulously, even more nettled than before. "Sorry to hear that—I had hoped that I had discovered something moderately important."

"So you did, Bill. But its importance was not exactly in reference to the actual murder."

"What on earth do you—"

"Its importance is a matter of accumulation—its real relation is to the boot-lace and the Barker I.O.U."

I shook my head hopelessly. "What can Mary's letter have to do with those other things—you said yourself we didn't know to whom the letter was written—besides, we have Mary's word that she never wrote to Prescott in her life—surely you believe her—you can't doubt her?"

"Not for a moment, Bill."

"Well, then"—I became emphatic—"there must be—"

"You'll see what I'm getting at all in good time. Don't be impatient—besides, here we are at 'The Swan's Nest.'"

The news of the inquest had excited considerable interest, and a good-sized knot of people had gathered outside the hostelry. As we entered, I heard speculation regarding many details of the case, and our identity was audibly discussed. Dr. Anselm was just taking his seat. He referred to the shocking nature of the tragedy that was to be there, and then investigated and proceeded at once to put the case before the twelve good men and true. Witnesses, he informed us, would be called to identify the deceased as Gerald Prescott, a guest of Sir Charles Considine—he mentioned the name with proper respect and reverence—at Considine Manor, where he had been staying for nearly a week. A good many of the company knew that the poor young man—with whose relatives he would desire to express his deepest sympathy—had appeared in the last 'Varsity Match at Lords', and had been invited to Considine Manor to take part in Sir Charles Considine's Annual Cricket Week. Nothing of any untoward incident had occurred during his stay—they had no evidence of any quarrelling or friction of any kind— yet on the Saturday morning, Prescott had been found lying on the billiard-table—in the—ahem—billiard room—foully murdered. *Sensation!* Done to death by strangulation, Dr. Elliott would inform them, as a highly qualified medical man, and it would be the jury's duty to weigh this evidence and all the evidence to arrive at a fit and proper verdict. In addition to a boot-lace tied tightly round his throat, the murdered man had also been stabbed at the base of the neck, at the top of the spinal cord with a dagger! *More and greater sensation!* The case had also a strange complication. On the night of the murder, Lady Considine's pearls had been stolen from the Manor. *Again sensation!* But owing to the masterly handling of this portion of the affair by Inspector Baddeley of the Sussex Constabulary, who had acted with lightning-like rapidity in the following up of certain data that he had gleaned, two persons had been arrested and lodged in Lewes Jail. *Final and crowning sensation!* The reporters present licked their lips. This was almost too good to be true. Anthony nudged me in the ribs. "He's rendered to Baddeley the things that weren't Baddeley's—you see!" He grinned. "Just as I expected."

Dr. Anselm speedily got to the real business of the morning. The room we were in was evidently the dining-room of the "Swan's Nest," and I attempted to picture it in its ordinary environment. It seemed grotesque to imagine people could dine here in any comfort after this inquiry was over. Then I heard "Mrs. Prescott" called.

The Coroner once again expressed his profound sympathy with her in her distress. She gave formal evidence identifying the body that she had viewed as the body of her son—Gerald Onslow Lancelot Prescott. He was twenty-two years of age—unmarried—and had just come down from Oxford. As far as she was aware deceased had no troubles or worries; he was quite sound financially and to her knowledge hadn't an enemy in the world.

*The Coroner.*—"Had he any love affair?"

*Mrs. Prescott.*—"No. None that he had ever confided to me."

*The Coroner.*—"He had come to Considine Manor simply to take part in the Cricket Week?"

*Mrs. Prescott.*—"That is so."

*The Coroner.*—"Had you heard from him during his stay there?"

*Mrs. Prescott.*—"Yes—a short letter. Full of the good times he was having."

*The Coroner.*—"And you know of absolutely nothing that would throw any light upon this indescribably dreadful affair?"

*Mrs. Prescott.*—"Nothing! Nothing at all!"

The Coroner thanked her and the next witness was summoned. If summoned can correctly describe the procedure.

"Constance Webb!"

From between two sturdy members of the Sussex County Police came she whom we had known as Marshall. *Still sensation!*

The reporters bent to their tasks with redoubled energy—sweetened by the thoughts of circulations to come. A low hum buzzed round the room at the appearance of this new witness. Anthony clutched at my arm.

"Look," he muttered. Inspector Baddeley had come round to the side of Dr. Anselm and was whispering something to him. I saw the Coroner nod his head three or four times in seeming acquiescence. Baddeley appeared to be explaining something, for I saw the doctor give a final approving movement of the head, and then turn and address the witness.

"What's afoot?" I interrogated.

"I think I know," answered Anthony. "Listen!"

"Marshall," as it seems the more natural for me to call her, gave her evidence in a low, toneless, almost inaudible voice. Several times the Coroner had to request her to speak up. Up to Saturday last she had been a maid in the employ of Sir Charles and Lady Considine, and among her duties was the task of sweeping and cleaning a number of the Manor rooms first thing in the morning—as she had done on the Saturday morning in question. She had eventually reached the billiard room! Here the witness was observed to falter and excitement ran high in the "Swan's Nest." Dr. Anselm took a hand.

"What did you find when you got to the billiard room?"

More excitement followed—a sharp-featured little man on the left of the room jumped to his feet. All eyes were turned on him.

"I object to that question, sir, with all deference—the witness has not yet said that she had found anything."

Dr. Anselm glared at this disturber of the peace. "Who are you, sir?"

The little man produced his card. "Felix Lawson. I am present at this inquiry watching the interests of Webb—the man under—"

The Coroner broke in quickly. "Very well, Mr. Lawson. That is sufficient."

He addressed himself to the witness again. "Tell your story—go on."

"I entered the billiard room and the first thing I saw was the dead body of Mr. Prescott lying across the billiard-table."

"What did you do?"

She hesitated for a brief period. "I screamed for help! Then the other people came in."

"I see! I will only ask you one more question. Describe the attitude of the body on the table as well as you are able."

"It seemed to be lying across the end of the table—almost on one shoulder—I can't remember any more. Is that all?"

Dr. Anselm asserted his satisfaction.

"Inspector Baddeley!" Baddeley stepped forward, as briskly as ever.

He told his story curtly and decisively. He explained that he had been called to Considine Manor about eight o'clock on the morning in question, in company with Dr. Elliott. As the previous witness had stated, the body of the dead man lay across the billiard-table in the billiard room. The room was to an extent disordered. Three of the chairs were overturned, and by the side of one lay the poker from the fireplace. The window of the room was open—probably about two feet. There were footprints outside this window, indicating that deceased had been out there, and another man as well. With regard to this latter fact he would say no more for the moment.

Anthony plucked at my elbow. "You'll hear no mention of the 'Spider'—you see."

Baddeley went on with his evidence. No money had been found on the deceased, although he was almost fully dressed. He was wearing, when discovered, full evening dress with the exception of his shoes. These were brown—the deceased had evidently pulled them on in a great hurry. He had made inquiries about the deceased gentleman, and had discovered nothing whatever to his discredit or detriment. Inspector Baddeley retired.

Dr. Elliott then followed with his medical testimony. Once again the room at the "Swan's Nest" buzzed and hummed with excitement. Death was due, he told his audience, to strangulation. Deceased had been strangled by a brown shoe-lace, taken from one of the shoes that he was wearing and tied tightly round his throat. A dagger had also been driven into the base of the neck, at the top of the spinal column, but in his opinion, death had already supervened before this assault had taken place. *Acute sensation!*

*A Juryman.*—"Was it possible, Dr. Elliott, for this shoe-lace to have been placed round deceased's neck by deceased himself?"

*Dr. Elliott.*—"You suggest suicide?"

*A Juryman.*—"Yes. That's what I mean."

*Dr. Elliott.*—"Quite possible, of course, but as a medical man, I hardly—"

*A Juryman.*—"Thank ye, Doctor."

Continuing, Dr. Elliott gave it his considered opinion that death had taken place about six or seven hours before he first examined the body.

*The Coroner.*—"That would time the murder then, Dr. Elliott, at about one o'clock or half-past? Am I correct?"

Dr. Elliott agreed. In conclusion he stated that the body he had examined was normal, and healthy in every respect—that of an athletic young man.

Then Anthony and I became like the crowd. We got *our* sensation.

"Andrew Whitney."

"Who the blazes is this?" I asked excitedly. "Somebody Baddeley has dug up?" Anthony leaned forward in his seat to look at the newcomer.

A medium-sized fat-faced man stepped up. He had a jovial, well-nourished countenance and was evidently full to the brim with *joie de vivre*. He gave his evidence very quickly and clearly.

"I am Andrew Whitney—Sales Manager, Blue Star Soap Products Co.—I was motoring home on Friday night last from Eastbourne. My home is at Coulsdon. I left Eastbourne very late—I had been staying with friends—and it was very probably Saturday morning before I actually got under way. To make matters worse I had engine trouble, and it was striking three as I came through Considine. I remember hearing two church clocks strike the hour. I passed Considine Manor about five minutes past three. Just as I was passing, the engine trouble that had previously helped to delay me, recurred and I was forced to stop again. While I was tinkering about at the job, I was surprised to see a room at the side of the house suddenly flash into brilliant light—the electric light was suddenly turned on. It remained on for a period that I should estimate at two or three minutes, and then equally suddenly went out. It struck me as rather strange that people should be walking about in rooms at that hour of the night. I have since identified that room where the light was, as the billiard room."

The man who had described himself as Felix Lawson rose to his feet. He bowed to the Coroner. "With your permission, Dr. Anselm, I would like to put one question to the witness."

"Very well, Mr. Lawson."

The little man turned to Whitney. "Are you prepared to affirm, on oath, Mr. Whitney, that this lighting up of the billiard room took place *after* three o'clock? You are absolutely certain of your time?"

Whitney nodded his head impatiently. "Quite positive. I imagined I had made myself clear on that point."

Lawson raised his hand deprecatingly. "You were judging, I think, from the chimes of a clock. They are very easily miscounted, especially when your mind is otherwise pretty well occupied. You *counted* the strokes and were *sure*?"

"I did. I am positive on the point."

"Thank you very much. Thank you, Dr. Anselm. That is all I have to ask."

Whitney stepped away smartly.

"Annie Dennis."

A girl whose face was vaguely familiar to me came forward. When she started to speak I realized that I knew her. It was one of the kitchen maids at the Manor. She had been called as a result of Inspector Baddeley's inquiries, and had something to tell the world which the Inspector considered important. I whispered again to Anthony Bathurst.

"Did you know about this?" I said.

"No," he replied. "Not a glimmer. The Inspector has been busy."

Annie's evidence was as follows. On Friday evening she had been sent down into the village by Fitch, the butler. She had returned just after nine o'clock, and as she entered the grounds of the Manor she was amazed to see a man walking on the flower-bed directly outside the billiard room window.

*Dr. Anselm.*—"What exactly did he appear to be doing?"

"Nothing! Only walking across the bed."

"Can you describe him?"

The witness shook her head. "No, sir—not very well. He seemed to disappear very quickly as I drew nearer to the house itself. But there was something a little peculiar about his walk."

"In what way peculiar?"

Annie Dennis hesitated. "I can't rightly say, sir, it just didn't seem ordinary-like—not free and easy."

"Do you mean that he limped in some way or was lame?"

"No, sir, not exactly that—I can't tell you quite what I mean—but I should know it if I ever saw it again."

Dr. Anselm desisted from worrying the witness any more, and having summed the whole facts up, concisely and accurately, the jury were asked for their verdict. It was speedily forthcoming. "Wilful Murder against some person or persons unknown—death having been caused by strangulation."

We filed out of the room one by one. I was anxious to ask Anthony his opinion of the two fresh witnesses. I turned to address him when I found, to my surprise, Inspector Baddeley at our sides.

"I'd like a chat with you, Mr. Bathurst," he said, "at your convenience."

"Whenever you like, Baddeley! You've deserted the 'Spider' then?"

"Not altogether, although it might appear to be so," came the answer.

"You must have strong reasons."

"Pretty fair," grinned the Inspector. Then his face relapsed into the grave again. "Still, I'm not denying that I'm puzzled," he admitted. "I can't get the facts to tally at all. That's why I want a word with you. Understand?"

Anthony patted him on the back. "Only too pleased, Inspector; the case has been rather troublesome, I admit." We walked home together.

## Chapter XVII

## INSPECTOR BADDELEY PUTS HIS CARDS ON THE TABLE

BADDELEY closed the library door behind us and gestured to us to be seated. "I don't purpose troubling Sir Charles Considine at the moment," he informed us, "for one or two reasons—but I do feel, gentlemen, that I've reached a stage in the investigations of this affair when I'm bound to talk things over with somebody." He paused and produced his pipe which he proceeded to fill, slowly and deliberately. Then he continued. "Early on, Mr. Bathurst, you had a little joke with me about going fifty-fifty in regard to our discoveries . . . well . . . it's like this . . . I seem to be properly up against the most baffling set of clues it's ever been my good fortune—or bad, if you like—to encounter." He struck a match and lit the tobacco. "In all probability I've been able to get information that you haven't, Mr. Bathurst—that sort of thing's my job so you're starting a bit 'scratch' as it were—still I'm going to play the game and put all the cards on the table."

Anthony waved a deprecating hand. "Quite so—Inspector."

Baddeley eyed him warily—then went on again.

"There's a young fellow murdered and a pearl necklace stolen in the same house on the same night. The robbery is cleared up pretty quickly—thanks to you, Mr. Bathurst—and the question arises—the natural question if I may call it so—what connection, if any, is there between the two?"

Anthony broke in. "Do you want me to answer that?"

Baddeley held up his hand. "Not for the moment, sir! Let me go on for a bit. My reason tells me that there is a connection—because the murdered man was strangled with a shoe-lace, and the man pinched for the robbery has, as far as I can tell—the identical shoe-lace in his pocket. I'm not exactly a scholar, gentlemen, but you can say he's caught 'in flagrante delicto.'" He looked at us.

Anthony was smiling. "Go ahead, Inspector," was all that he said.

"Well, sir—that's what reason tells me! But instinct tells me just the opposite—I can't get the times to fit—nothing seems to link up just in the way that it should—and I've got a decidedly uneasy feeling that I've missed my way somewhere." He puffed at his pipe. "I'm going to do a lot of talking, gentlemen; can you put up with it?" He proceeded without waiting for our reply.

"Usually, there's a motive sticking out in these cases. But I'm damned if I can find a really satisfactory one here. Robbery? I don't think so—he had no money on him when he was found—but his chief card winnings hadn't been paid over, and it isn't likely he was carrying a very large sum about with him. Robbery for something that he possessed? The I.O.U. for instance? Possibly! Revenge? Again—possibly! But if so for something that has, so far, eluded me. Still—we'll concede—a distinct possibility. You see—we aren't nearing probabilities yet. And probabilities are much more satisfactory than mere possibilities. Now there's that very mysterious piece of work with the Venetian Dagger."

He stopped again as though to let his words sink well in. Anthony grew very attentive, and I found myself more responsive, so to speak, to the Inspector's mood.

"The dagger had been used to 'make sure' apparently. The murderer was taking no risks—dead men tell no tales—but—and here's something you probably don't know, Mr. Bathurst—that Venetian dagger had unmistakable signs of finger-prints."

Anthony grinned. "It was the dagger, after all, Bill," he said. Then he addressed Baddeley. "I tumbled to your letter dodge, Inspector," he explained. "I spotted that you had some prints somewhere and were after an identification. Fire away." He settled in his chair again. Baddeley gazed at him steadily.

"You miss a hell of a lot. I *don't* think," he muttered. "I fancy I've brought my samples to the right market, after all."

Anthony dismissed the compliment with a wave of the hand. Then came as quickly to the challenging point. "Whose were they?"

Baddeley replied very quietly. "They belonged to Major Hornby, Mr. Bathurst."

This was interesting with a vengeance.

"Really," said Anthony. "This is very important! Have you approached the Major, or are you holding your hand?"

"I have seen the Major, and informed him of my knowledge."

"Ah! I am curious to hear what he says."

"His explanation is that he handled the dagger during the evening."

"Really."

"Yes. And what is more, Mr. Bathurst, he is prepared to assert that when he retired for the night, the dagger had been removed from its customary resting-place on the table."

"Removed from where he had replaced it?"

"Exactly."

Anthony looked up and studied the Inspector's face very seriously. "Really—Inspector. Really? This is most illuminating! Taken from the table some time during the evening—eh?" He rubbed his hands. "And do you know, Inspector—do you know—I'm not surprised."

Baddeley flung him a quizzical glance. "The day that I surprise you, I reckon I'll surprise myself," he uttered laconically. "But I'll go on. I've given you one piece of information that I believe you were ignorant of. Now for what happened this morning at the inquest—I fancy you heard a thing or two there for the first time? Am I right?"

Anthony pulled at his top lip with his fingers—a favourite trick of his. "You refer to the evidence of Andrew Whitney and the maid, Dennis—I presume?"

Baddeley nodded. "Whitney's evidence was a stroke of pure good fortune for me. He had seen the account of the case in the papers, read the description of the house, Considine Manor, and knowing of course that his delay occurred in the village of Considine or thereabouts, had no difficulty in recognizing it again when he came to have a second look at it. I tell you I was glad to get my hooks into this piece of evidence, from an absolutely unimpeachable source—but when he swore that the time was past three—well, I was pretty well staggered." He came right across to us and looked Anthony straight in the face. "Mr. Bathurst, think it over! Dr. Elliott tells us Prescott was killed somewhere about half-past one—perhaps two—'Spider' Webb was pulling off his little job of work round about the same time—it all seems to point to a connection between the two—yet I'm not satisfied—I can't think what was doing in that billiard room after three o'clock that morning." He stared broodingly at his pipe. Neither Anthony nor I broke the silence—he seemed determined to let Baddeley have his entire say without further interruption.

"So much then for Whitney's evidence. Now we come to Annie Dennis. I am indebted to the butler—Fitch—for getting on to her. When I first questioned her she told me she could tell me nothing. Apparently she had either forgotten the incident or didn't consider it of sufficient importance to mention. She took it to Fitch who passed it on to me—so I interviewed her. What was a man doing outside the billiard room window at that time—just after nine o'clock—on Friday evening? Once again—was it Webb—or an accomplice of Webb's? There are too many twists and turns in this for me, Mr. Bathurst. I'm fairly staggered."

Anthony rose and stretched his long body.

"This inquest to-day, Inspector Baddeley—I was very interested to observe that all reference to Webb's arrest was avoided. In fact, as far as I can remember not a great deal of mention was made of the theft of Lady Considine's necklace. Marshall—Mrs. Webb—was treated exactly as an ordinary witness. I presume I am correct, Inspector, in assuming that you stage-managed this?"

Baddeley smiled. "Right again, Mr. Bathurst!"

"May I ask why? I have my own ideas of course—but—"

Baddeley cut in. "Well, I'll be perfectly frank with you, Mr. Bathurst. In these cases as you are doubtless aware, especially at an inquest, it isn't always the best policy for the Police to put all their cards on the table—at first that is. The robbery and the murder may be linked up—on the other hand they may not—if they are not—as my instinct tells me—it's just as well for the real murderer to remain in the dark about Webb."

Anthony pondered for a moment. "All very well, as far as it goes. To have charged Webb and Marshall with the murder might possibly have given this other chap—your murderer—a sense of false security. Don't you think so?"

"I always believe in keeping people uninformed—as far as possible. They are more likely to betray themselves."

"But there is an alternative to that," replied Anthony. "By imparting information—carefully prepared and selected, you sometimes force people to betray themselves. Don't you see? However, it's of no particular consequence—I merely desired to know what exactly was your intention. Now I know!"

Baddeley plunged his hands into his jacket pockets. "You asked me just now, Mr. Bathurst, if I wanted you to answer a question that I had raised—and I asked you to refrain from answering it at the moment. I'd like you to answer it now. Has Webb with his robbery any connection with the death of Prescott?"

"You want me to answer that—here and now?"

"If you please, Mr. Bathurst."

"In my opinion, then, as I read the case, none whatever!"

"None whatever!"—I intervened incredulously—"then what about the shoe-lace? I can't understand—"

"Neither can I," reiterated Baddeley. "That beats me—that does."

Anthony smiled. "You asked me a simple question, and I gave you a simple answer. Let's leave it at that, for the time being. And now allow me to ask you a question!"

Baddeley signified assent. "Very well, sir!"

"Shortly after you were called to this business, Inspector—you definitely stated that Prescott had been out in the grounds of the Manor *after* twelve o'clock. Do you remember?"

"Decidedly, I do," came the answer. "What are you getting at?"

"You drew your inference, I supposed, Inspector, from the mud on the brown shoes, and the state of the clothes that Prescott was wearing when found? They were bone-dry, and you argued that had he been out before twelve they would have got very wet—rain was falling pretty steadily—and would still have shown some traces of wet when you arrived. Am I on the lines of your reasoning?"

"You are—pretty conclusive too, don't you think?"

"It would fit one hypothesis, certainly—but not another."

"I don't quite get you."

"Don't go too fast. I was merely satisfying myself as to the line your inferences had taken."

Baddeley looked doubtfully at him. "You think I've missed something?"

Anthony patted him on the shoulder. "Naturally—we all have, haven't we—or the murderer would be kicking his heels in Lewes Jail by this time—there's no urgent necessity for you to be despondent because of that."

"That's all very well," returned the Inspector—"but you see this happens to be my job—my bread and butter depends on it—I can't afford to miss things and get away with it."

"Don't abandon hope yet," responded Anthony. "I am becoming more optimistic as we progress. You'll clap your handcuffs on the criminal yet. Now tell me something else. You collared Prescott's papers when you first ran your eye over his bedroom. Find anything?"

"Nothing of any consequence. Here they are." He fished in his breast pocket. Then produced an ordinary brown leather wallet which he handed over to my companion. About a shilling's worth of postage stamps, and half a dozen papers were all it contained. Anthony looked through them.

"Hotel Bill—July—'Varsity Match probably, two letters from his mother"—he scanned them through—"not important—a communication from the O.U.D.S.—another from the 'Authentics'—and a tailor's bill. H'm—nothing here apparently." He returned the wallet to Baddeley.

"Did you get his check-book?"

"You bet your life I did. Care to have a look at that?" He smiled.

Anthony turned over the counterfoils for a moment or two. "Nothing here, either, I fancy; only five checks drawn since the beginning of May—four to 'Self' and one to the tailor whose account we just handled. Well, I'm not surprised—I didn't want to find anything startling."

"Any information helps," muttered Baddeley somewhat gloomily.

"Not always, Inspector! Consider your own position here—you found pieces of information from time to time that only served to confuse you. You have admitted that yourself! They wouldn't fit in, as links in the chain—I had the same difficulty—"

"That's true," conceded the Inspector. "But you like to feel you're running freely."

Anthony went straight across to him. "I do, Inspector. I feel that I'm actually 'in the straight.'"

But Baddeley refused to be comforted. "I'm not denying that you've done one or two smart things, but I'm afraid you're a bit over-confident. I've been at the game longer than—"

Anthony cut in. "Look here, Baddeley, do you think I should say a thing like that, without good and sufficient reason?"

I subjected Baddeley to a careful scrutiny, for I felt myself sympathizing with him. How could Anthony possibly make a statement like that? It seemed to me from what I had seen of the case—which was as much as anybody—that several people lay under suspicion, but none more than any other. Now there was Hornby to add to Webb, Barker, "Marshall" and the rest of them. I could quite see Baddeley's point of view—a maze of clues and not one, to my outlook, that stood out conspicuously from the others.

Baddeley's voice broke in upon my reverie.

"No, Mr. Bathurst—I don't! But since you ask me—I'm dashed if I can follow you—I *don't* see my way clearly and that's a fact."

Anthony took a cigarette from his case—we did likewise at his invitation. "Do you mind being the third, Inspector?" he asked as we lit up.

"I'm not superstitious, Mr. Bathurst—though I've a shrewd idea this little conference will prove unlucky for somebody." We laughed.

"You do?" said Anthony. "Well, listen to me for a moment."

## CHAPTER XVIII
## MR. BATHURST PARTIALLY EMULATES HIS EXAMPLE

WE SETTLED down in our chairs, eager and expectant. I think Baddeley shared my feelings now. What were we going to hear that would throw light on the affair?

"You've acted very decently all the way through, Baddeley, I'll say that for you, and I appreciate it as a compliment that we're running this little 'confab' now. I realize that to a certain extent, you have come to me for help—well, I'll give you some. You said just now you were going to put your cards on the table. Perhaps you thought that I held some trumps too." He paused and waited for the Inspector to reply. But the answer was some little time in coming. Baddeley shifted uneasily in his seat as though he didn't altogether approve of Anthony's opening remarks. Then somewhat grudgingly it seemed to me he answered the question that had been put to him.

"Well—perhaps I did, Mr. Bathurst." Then, as though he realized partly that he was exposing himself to charge of churlishness, he made the *amende*.

"You see, Mr. Bathurst, I've developed a certain amount of admiration for you."

Anthony smiled. "Then we know where and how we stand. In the first place, Inspector—a question. When were you last in the billiard room?"

"Yesterday—Wednesday."

"Care for a jaunt up there now? I'll show you something."

Baddeley looked surprised, but accepted the invitation with alacrity. We ascended the stairs—I knew well what the journey meant for us.

"Billiards"—said Anthony, with an air—"have lapsed into disfavour since Prescott was found murdered. A very natural consequence, I submit. Sir Charles and Jack have kept away, Arkwright has had a nasty attack of muscular rheumatism in his right arm—Mary Considine and Helen have given the room a miss. But Bill and I fancied a game. I fancy it was on Tuesday. Shortly after we started—one of us potted the red rather brilliantly—modesty prevents me telling you which of us it was, Inspector—are you interested?"

Baddeley eyed him studiously—but refrained from replying.

"That was the pocket"—he indicated it—"where the balls are now. Do you mind putting your hand in and sending them out? Thank you, Inspector. Now feel in the pocket."

I watched Baddeley's look of amazement as he thrust in his hand. Barker's I.O.U. was still lying where we had replaced it. He took it and smoothed it out, his look of amazement deepening.

"You found this here?" he gasped. "When? Why didn't you tell me before?"

"Come now, Inspector. Recriminations weren't part of our bargain. We found this, Cunningham and I, exactly as I have indicated—I am not pretending that I found it because I was looking for it—it was entirely fortuitous."

Baddeley made no reply. He read and reread the writing. Then tapping it with his forefinger: "Here's the motive—gentlemen. The very link for which I've been searching. Prescott was murdered for possession of this I.O.U., and the murderer in his haste or excitement dropped or lost the very object he wanted to obtain." Then to us—"don't you think so?"

"I ought to tell you, Inspector," Anthony answered, "that I don't quite know the actual position that this piece of envelope was occupying in the pocket when I found it. Don't look mystified! I sent the balls flying from the pocket with the flat of my hand, *before* I discovered the I.O.U. Therefore, you understand, I don't know for certain if it was down the side of the pocket say—or right at the bottom—*under* the billiard balls! Get me?"

"Yes, I understand that. You think the paper's position important?"

"Very. For instance, if I could definitely assert that it occupied the latter position, I should incline to the opinion that it had been *hidden* there—not accidentally dropped."

Baddeley rubbed the ridge of his jaw with his knuckles.

"Yes—that's sound reasoning," he admitted. "But why hide it? Why murder to get it—and then hide it? That beats me—it does."

"It wants a bit of working out," chuckled Anthony. "Still, there's nothing more to be gained by staying up here. Hang on to that precious piece of paper and let's get back to the library."

Baddeley followed us out of the room.

"On second thoughts," interposed Anthony, "come upstairs once more and not down. Come on, Bill. Come on, Baddeley. There's something else I want to tell you."

He showed the way to Prescott's bedroom, while Baddeley trailed along in apparent discomfiture.

"You'll not be able to hand me out any surprise packets in here, Mr. Bathurst. I went through Prescott's belongings pretty thoroughly."

"I'll give you credit for that," laughed Anthony. "So don't worry on that score. I'm going to take you farther than this room—but only just a little farther. Come into the bathroom."

We made our way—I bringing up the rear. Anthony fished in his pocket and produced the cigar stub that he had so carefully preserved. He passed it on to our companion. "See that cigar end, Baddeley? That was found on the edge of this wash-stand basin—I found it there, and on this occasion I *do* know where it was lying." He pointed to the spot. "And I'll tell you this"—he continued. "As far as either of us can say—we don't think it's one of Sir Charles Considine's—it's certainly not one of his customary brand."

"Been smoked by a man with jolly good teeth," remarked the Inspector as he studied it closely. "Prescott himself had excellent teeth—gentlemen."

"Yes—that's a distinct possibility—I admit that," replied Anthony. "Just a piece of absent-mindedness on his part might account for its presence there."

Baddeley nodded. "Was he a cigar smoker? Can you tell me?"

"What do you mean?" I broke in. "Habitually—or occasionally?"

"Either!"

"Well," I uttered, "he'd smoke a cigar after dinner if Sir Charles or anybody offered him one—I can tell you that—I've often seen him."

"Just so! That's all I meant. I'll keep this and make a few inquiries."

"By the way, Baddeley"—from Anthony—"you went all over the bedroom itself pretty systematically—didn't you?"

"I did that," replied Baddeley. "And I don't think I missed anything."

It was on the tip of my tongue to put him wise again—I thought of the letter fragments—but Anthony put a quick finger to his lips, unseen by the Inspector. I also caught the fleeting suggestion of a lowered eyelid. It then became evident to me that he did not intend to let Baddeley know what I had found in the bedroom. Neither had he mentioned Mary's evidence about the mysterious watcher that she and Prescott had seen— in short, I realized that Anthony was only putting some of his cards on the table.

Baddeley led the way downstairs somewhat ruefully, I thought.

"I must thank you, Mr. Bathurst, for putting me wise on these points," he said very frankly. "But if I was to say that I felt any nearer to a solution, because of them—well—I shouldn't be taking a medal for veracity. Think I'd better start keeping rabbits. More in my line."

"Don't be too self-critical, Inspector. A little is good for all of us—but a little goes a long way, and too much of it is bad for one."

Inspector Baddeley looked at him with no little chagrin.

"You mean what you say, kindly, I've no doubt, but I feel that I'd like to think quietly over what I've learned from you to-day. Somewhere, at my leisure—I get a bit bewildered unless I can go my own pace. So you won't mind if I say 'good-day'?" He held out his hand to us in farewell. "Good-day, Mr. Bathurst! Good-day, Mr. Cunningham!"

Anthony looked after him whimsically as he closed the door. Then we heard Sir Charles Considine's voice booming out. "Hullo, Baddeley, what did you think of old Anselm? The inquest didn't produce much that we didn't know—eh—and also didn't produce some that we did—what?" Baddeley appeared to murmur a reply that tickled Sir Charles' humour.

"Very good. Very good! What do you think of that, Jack—eh, Arkwright?—good-bye, Baddeley."

"Good-day, Sir Charles." We heard the Inspector's footsteps down the drive. I turned to Anthony.

"You deliberately kept Mary's evidence from him, and you didn't show him those letter fragments I found in the bedroom. Why?"

"Why? Well, I told him as much as I thought was good for him to know!"

"It seems hardly fair to him," I muttered. "He's handicapped."

"Less than if I hadn't told him what I did. I've helped him. For instance he's got the Barker I.O.U. and the cigar stub. He'll probably get to work on the latter at once."

This last remark was a wonderfully good shot on Anthony's part. For Inspector Baddeley went straight into the village to the larger of the two tobacconists that supplied Considine and its adjoining district with its nicotine needs. This establishment was kept by a large florid-faced man—Abbott, by name. Baddeley handed over the object of inquiry.

"Could you possibly tell me what brand of cigar this is, Mr. Abbott?"

Abbott took it, after the manner of a connoisseur. Felt it—then smelt it. Then shook his head. "Afraid not, sir. But it's just a common one. Quite ordinary—what we in the trade would call a four-penny or five-penny smoke—sold in a 'pub' very likely. But I couldn't give the brand a name."

"I see! Sold many yourself lately?"

Abbott's answer was a decided negative.

"Don't sell a cigar once a week now, down here! It's all tobacco and cigarettes with the villagers. Afraid I can't help you there."

The Inspector thanked him and withdrew.

"Drawn a blank there," he muttered to himself, dismally. He weighed the matter over in his mind. Should he pursue that line of investigation any farther? It seemed to him that it would prove, in all probability, a fruitless one. He might go to a dozen places and fail to find anything definite about a cigar like this—it might have been purchased a hundred miles away. Again it might prove nothing—it might have been, as he had been quick enough to point out—Prescott's own—just left on the wash-stand basin carelessly. He decided to abandon it. Then the question of the I.O.U. obtruded itself again. One thing, he knew whose that was! On second thoughts that should prove very much more profitable if followed up. Confronted by that—Lieutenant Malcolm Barker might, conceivably, tell a different story. Major Hornby, too! Try as he would, he couldn't entirely rid his mind of the suspicion that that gentleman knew more than he had so far been disposed to tell.

Baddeley squared his shoulders and thrust his hands into his pockets. He would lose no time in seeing both Barker and Hornby again. This time they would find him very much more determined. Especially Major Hornby—damn him!

# CHAPTER XIX
# MR. BATHURST'S WONDERFUL SYMPATHY

ANTHONY DRAINED his last cup of tea and pushed his chair away from the breakfast table.

"Fitch!" He called the butler over to his side. Fitch listened to him.

"Yes, sir. With pleasure. I think it's the July issue. I will obtain it for you, sir; in just a moment!"

I think the rest of the company were somewhat surprised to see the excellent Fitch return with the A.B.C.

"Leaving us, Bathurst?" queried Sir Charles Considine. "You haven't forgotten our—?"

"No, sir. Only taking a run up to town. I shall be back this evening."

"Want a companion?" I asked.

He thought for a moment or two. "Awfully good of you, Bill—but if you don't mind, I'll go alone. I'm not altogether sure that I shan't be wasting my time—so I've no desire to waste yours, possibly!" He smiled his disarming smile. I was immediately mollified.

"Have the Morris-Oxford, Bathurst, to run you to the station," offered Sir Charles.

"Thank you very much, sir, I shall be delighted. I'll leave here about twenty minutes past ten. I'll just go and get ready."

"What's taking him away, Bill?" said Jack Considine. "I'm not inquisitive I hope, but is it this Prescott business?"

"I can't say," I replied. "Very probably, though."

"I think it must be," announced Sir Charles. "Baddeley was up here again yesterday, you know. I had a moment with him. I gave him a rub or two concerning the inquest." He chuckled. "He's a very decent fellow though, and very despondent at the moment over his lack of success in regard to, what I am informed, is now known to the world in general as 'The Billiard Room Mystery.'" He sighed. "Such is fame, Helen! Anyhow, when I realized that he was genuinely sore and upset, I tried a different tack. I'm afraid this case would have tried a greater brain than Baddeley's."

"Well, I for one, sincerely hope the affair will be settled," intervened Captain Arkwright. "We are all more or less under a cloud while it remains unsolved—that's how I feel about it. And others besides us—Hornby, Tennant, Daventry—and all the fellows that were here at the time."

"That's very true," agreed our host. "The whole house is under a cloud—the Cricket Week will always have this unholy reminiscence hanging over it—even after the whole tangle is cleared away—if it ever is cleared away. Of course there is less strain for all of us since Mrs. Prescott returned to London."

The door opened and Anthony came quickly in.

"The car's waiting, sir, so with your permission, I'll get away."

He waved a good-bye and shortly afterwards we heard the car go humming away down the road. He reached the station with a good five minutes to spare before his train (as he related afterwards) so he sauntered to the booking office to get his ticket. Surely he knew that figure just in advance of him!

"Good-morning, Inspector!" Baddeley wheeled quickly at the unexpected greeting.

"Why, it's Mr. Bathurst. Going to Victoria, sir?"

"Yes. Are you?"

"Thought of taking a run up." He grinned. "Though I didn't know I was coming till this morning, itself."

"Good! We'll travel together then, Inspector."

The train rumbled in and the pair sought, with success, an empty compartment.

Baddeley was in a communicative mood.

"Major Hornby has left Canterbury, Mr. Bathurst. You may be interested to know that. I made inquiries last night. He's stopping at a private hotel in the Kensington district—near Gloucester Road."

Mr. Bathurst was interested—but not tremendously. He was not aware of the Inspector's desire to get into touch again with Major Hornby. How had the Inspector fared over the little matter of the cigar stub?

"A dead end, Mr. Bathurst!"

Mr. Bathurst complimented his companion upon the particular aptness of his reply, but was assured with transparent sincerity that it had been unintentional. How far had the Inspector taken the line of his investigation?

"It was a commonplace brand of cigar—sold most probably in a 'pub'—to trace it would entail a long and arduous task—and then might prove to be unilluminative. I abandoned the idea!"

Then the Inspector was not at work on it this morning?

"No, as I indicated, I'm desirous of having another interview with Major Hornby. Are you leaving Considine for good?"

Mr. Bathurst was most certainly doing nothing of the kind. He was merely paying a visit to a friend. He was returning to Considine that evening—all being well.

"A great weight of what I will term—*police* opinion is in favour of charging Webb and his wife with the murder of Mr. Prescott. Up to the moment I have stalled them off. I don't think Webb's the man. That shoe-lace business doesn't spell Webb to my way of thinking, and as for the lace found in the 'Spider's' pocket—one lace is very like another."

Mr. Bathurst assented. But was rather surprised that Webb had *not* yet been charged with the murder.

"I'm not denying that a very strong 'prima facie' case could be made against him," said Baddeley—"because it undoubtedly could."

"Had Webb an alibi from any time of the fatal night?" asked Mr. Bathurst.

"Yes, he's attempted to put one forward from about two-fifteen. He states that he was with a confederate—so it comes from a source that is suspect—a good counsel would speedily demolish it."

Mr. Bathurst agreed. But there was Andrew Whitney to be considered. His evidence would help Webb considerably. He considered it was very sporting of Inspector Baddeley to have put him up before the Coroner.

Inspector Baddeley was not oblivious to the compliment and smiled his acknowledgment.

Then Mr. Bathurst took a turn.

Had the Inspector by any chance a photograph of the body when found? He believed he was correct in his idea that the Inspector had ordered Roper to take certain photographs of the room and body on that first morning.

Mr. Bathurst was quite right in his assumption, and Inspector Baddeley would be delighted to show him what he had. He produced half a dozen plates.

Mr. Bathurst examined them carefully. The Inspector offered his help. Was there any point in the disposition of the body upon which he could throw any further light?

Mr. Bathurst thanked him, but replied in the negative. He was not concerned about the position of the body. He was curious about the position of the red ball!

The Inspector stared in amazement. The red ball was not on the table! What on earth did Mr. Bathurst mean?

Mr. Bathurst quite understood that the red ball was not on the table because it was in the pocket as shown by one of the photographs taken from a higher altitude. He pointed it out to the Inspector—lying on top of the other two. By the time they reached Victoria, Inspector Baddeley was more perplexed than ever. "This is where we part, Inspector," said Anthony, as they passed through the barrier. "*Au'voir.*"

Anthony made his way to the underground and booked to Cannon Street. Arrived there he made tracks for the Main station.

The next train to Blackheath was at 12.22.

"That will land me there just in time for lunch," he thought to himself, and events proved him to be a sound prophet.

A smart-looking maid took the card he proffered her, and in a few seconds he found himself in what was evidently the drawing-room.

Mrs. Prescott followed him in. "I got your wire, Mr. Bathurst, and of course, I am very pleased to see you. I can hardly realize yet all that has happened. I'm trying to bear up—but frankly, I have little left in the world now to capture either my interest or my imagination. Now, what is it you wanted to see me about?"

Anthony was all sympathy. "I want to talk to you about your boy."

"You asked me a good many questions at Considine Manor, Mr. Bathurst. You wish to ask me some more?"

"If you would be kind enough to answer them."

Mrs. Prescott bowed her head in assent.

"First of all, let me assure you that I feel a very great sympathy with you in your sorrow." He touched her arm for a brief moment, very gently. "And I have every hope that the crime which has hurt you so much will not go unpunished." He spoke with a feeling that Mrs. Prescott was not slow to detect.

"I thank you for your words and for your sympathy, too, Mr. Bathurst."

"Tell me about your boy—as much as you can—everything!"

It was not a difficult thing that he had asked her.

A mother who has lost her boy—under the circumstances that she had—grasps at the straws of reminiscence to save herself from going under.

"Begin at the beginning," said Anthony.

She told him. He listened attentively. She got to his cricket—he had played for Oxford at Lords'.

Then Anthony made his first interruption.

"Tell me, Mrs. Prescott—has your son in any game or sport—been ambidextrous?"

Mrs. Prescott showed signs of surprise.

"Think carefully," he reiterated. "Did he ever bat left-handed or bowl left-handed—did he ever play billiards, for instance, left-handed?"

She shook her head. "Never to my knowledge, Mr. Bathurst."

"Had he any personal peculiarities, at all?"

"Peculiarities? Well, I suppose every one of us has a—"

"I mean physical. For example—a right-handed acquaintance of mine always counts money with his left hand and deals cards in the same way."

"I see what you mean," she declared. She thought, but to no effect.

"No, Mr. Bathurst, I can't think of anything like that."

Anthony accepted the situation, and Mrs. Prescott continued her memories.

"I can't imagine anything more that I can tell you," she concluded very quietly.

"Thank you very much. One last point. Had your son any particular knowledge of knots? The various types of knots that can be tied, that is?"

"Once again—not that I know of," she answered. "I think the only knot that I have ever seen him tie—was just an ordinary bow. Why do you ask?"

"A little whim of mine, Mrs. Prescott. Nothing more." He rose.

"You'll stay to lunch, Mr. Bathurst. I insist."

Anthony did, and when about to take his departure sometime afterwards realized that his hostess was a singularly able woman.

He shook hands with her. "Good-bye, Mr. Bathurst. You have hopes?"

"I have," he said gravely. "And fears. We are on the verge of a very horrible discovery. But it can't be helped. Good-bye."

Mrs. Prescott looked white and troubled as he spoke. "Good-bye," she murmured.

Anthony made off down the road—a prey to conflicting thoughts. Then he encountered a surprise, that quickly jolted him back to realities. Two figures passed by on the other side; well in his view. He stared in surprise. Major Hornby and Lieutenant Barker! "What the devil—" He stopped in the shadow of a wall and watched them curiously. They knocked at and entered the house that he had just left!

"Now—what on earth," he muttered. A hand touched him on the arm, and a voice exclaimed eagerly: "Tell me—quickly—whose house is that, Mr. Bathurst?" The hand was the hand of the Law—and the voice the voice of Inspector Baddeley.

# Chapter XX
# MARY RECEIVES HER SECOND
# PROPOSAL

WHEN ANTHONY left us that morning there was much speculation as to where he had gone and deny it as I might, I am pretty
certain that the company generally regarded me as being in his
confidence.

"What's his game, Bill?" demanded Arkwright. "You must
know—from—what's the correct term—information received."

I declared my ignorance. "Bathurst has not told me his
destination—and what's more, I haven't asked him. I told Jack
just now I knew nothing of his movements or intentions—for
to-day! He has, of course, confided one or two matters to me
during the past few days. I think, perhaps, I've helped him a
bit—once or twice."

I spoke with a sense of pride.

"Well, I for one, wish him success," cut in Jack Considine,
crisply. "Gerry Prescott was one of the best. A thunderin' good
all-round sportsman, and we can ill afford to lose him. I tell you
I'm more than sorry that he's gone—there are plenty of fellows
the world could have spared before Gerry Prescott! I know we
shall miss him in the 'House.'"

This outburst of Jack's startled me somewhat, and I noticed
Helen Arkwright and her husband look at him curiously.

Sir Charles himself, also seemed a trifle taken aback.

"Seems to me we have to wait till we're dead—to be thoroughly appreciated," I put in.

"Something like that, Bill," said Mary. "I've noticed that."

She rose and went into the garden. To me she had grown more
lovely than ever, during the past few days. The blow that had
befallen Considine Manor, and the sorrow that it had brought
in its train, seemed to have invested Mary with a serener beauty.
It was almost as though the charming winsomeness of the maid
had merged into the more steadfast beauty of the woman. The
sadness and sorrow had hastened the hand of Time. It was borne

upon me at that moment, that Life to me meant Mary Considine, and I determined to put into active form a resolution that had been but a thought to me for many months past.

I found her in the garden.

"The roses are going off, Bill," she said—pointing to the rose trees. "What a pity they don't last two or three months longer."

I looked at them. "Tell me their names, Mary?"

"Sharman Crawford, Caroline Testout, Daily Mail, La France, Betty, Xavier—"

I interrupted her. "Some roses are always with us," I ventured.

"Why, what do you mean, Bill?"

"I meant you," I replied. Lamely, I'm afraid. It sounded so, at least.

She smiled very sweetly. "That's very nice of you, Bill. I hope you really meant it."

"Of course I meant it. I never meant anything half so much in my life before."

"You mustn't make me conceited, Bill—and I'm afraid you will if you talk like that."

"I couldn't make you anything," I declared. "Only a master could make you, and I'm only a big lump of commonplaceness and ordinariness. You're just lovely. And to me, Mary, the loveliest, dearest and sweetest girl in the world,—for I love you."

"Oh, Bill," she gasped.

I caught her by the hand. "I want you to marry me, Mary. After all, I've got some little right to ask you. I've watched you grow up, you know. Give me the right to watch you grow up always."

I watched her face anxiously. And I fancied I saw her sweeping lashes brim with tiny tears. "Tell me—you will, darling?" I urged.

"This is very sudden, Bill—I know that sounds silly—but I can't think of anything else to say—and it's very dear of you to think so much of me."

"Then you *will*?" I said with eagerness.

"I don't know, Bill. I'm not quite sure. Of course, I like you—as we all do—but—"

I tried to take her in my arms but she evaded me.

"There's no one else—?" I asked. "Say there's no one else!"

"No." She spoke very quietly. "You may be easy on that point. There is no one else."

"Then why do you hesitate, dear? Put me out of my misery!"

"You must give me a little time to think it over, Bill." She held out her hand to me, and I took it.

"How long, Mary? How long? It isn't as though I'm a stranger to you."

"Not very long, Bill. I'll promise that. I just want to feel *sure*— you know."

She broke away and left me.

The rest of the day passed miserably for me. Anthony's absence didn't make it any the brighter and Mary's reception of my proposal had left me in an agony of apprehension. One moment I rose to heaven's heights and "struck the stars with my uplifted head"—the next found me in the depths of an intolerable despair. But generally, I was able to find courage and with courage—optimism! "There is no one else," she had said. Perhaps I had tried her too closely after Prescott and Prescott's death. "There is no one else!" Prescott belonged to the past tense. Would she have said that a week ago? I pondered the whole thing over in my mind. And the wondering with its attachment of doubt and uncertainty brought me the alternating moods that I have just described.

So the day wore on to the evening and dinner. Anthony had not returned, and everybody seemed very quiet. The meal passed uneventfully and conversation was desultory. I watched Mary carefully, trying to read my answer in her face. She seemed cheerful and smiling. Jack and Arkwright went into the drawing-room together, and in the buzz of their conversation I caught Prescott's name. The girls started music and we settled down comfortably. All the Considines have good voices, and they were always well worth listening to. After a time, Jack Considine and Arkwright strolled into the garden, but I refused the invitation to accompany them. I was thinking about Mary.

Suddenly two revolver shots rang out on the evening air. Shots that were succeeded by shouts.

Captain Arkwright came running up.

"Somebody's tried to murder Jack," he shouted. "In cold blood. Two shots have been fired at him from the direction of the Allingham Road. Great Scott! it was a near thing and no mistake. One has gone clean through his hat." He paused and wiped his face—pale with anxiety and worry.

"Where is Jack?" cried Lady Considine. "Are you sure he's all right?"

"He's coming. And he's all right—by the mercy of Providence. But what does it all mean?"

"Where were you, Arkwright?" demanded Sir Charles. "Weren't you with him?"

"No! I had left him for a moment. I stopped behind one of the trees on the way to the tennis courts to light a cigarette. There's a strong wind blowing."

"And Jack had walked on?"

"Yes, Jack was a couple of dozen paces ahead of me. Just as I was in the act of lighting up, my attention fully taken up—I heard two shots—revolver shots, I knew with certainty. I saw Jack spin round in amazement—his hat had been neatly drilled."

"A merciful escape," murmured Sir Charles.

"A merciful escape indeed, sir," replied Arkwright. "Then Jack shouted and I shouted—and I rushed back to tell you. He's coming along."

I ran into Jack some distance from the house. He looked a bit rattled and nervy, but was otherwise none the worse for the adventure.

"Been having a Wild West display, William," he grinned, when I met him. "Some enterprising blighter has succeeded in letting daylight into my best hat." He held out his soft hat to me. "Look!"

"What the devil's the matter with the place?" I growled. "Not much peaceful Sussex about it now. Who was it—any idea?"

"Not on your life, Bill," he responded. "All I know is that the beggar popped at me from the Allingham direction. And very nearly got me!" He paused and grasped me by the shoulder. "Considine Manor doesn't seem to be a health resort these days."

"Did you make any attempt to discover who it was?" I asked him.

"Well, for the moment I was too scared. When I did recover my presence of mind there wasn't a sign of anybody."

We reached the others. Sir Charles was bursting with indignation at this fresh outrage, but Lady Considine seemed more thankful at Jack's miraculous escape than upset at the shock. She fussed over him—mother-like.

"I suppose it's useless sending a search party out now?" fumed Sir Charles, "but by all the powers, I'll put Baddeley on to this in the morning!"

"Baddeley?" said a well-known voice. "What's Baddeley wanted for now?"

Sir Charles wheeled round quickly. His face lighted with relief.

"Another dastardly outrage, Bathurst! And in my own grounds, too!"

He proceeded to relate the incident. Anthony listened to him, gravely.

"Not more than a quarter of an hour ago, eh? I can't have missed it by much—I've just got back." He turned to Jack Considine.

"Tell me all the facts!"

Jack, assisted by Arkwright, retailed the whole story again.

"Come and show me the exact places you occupied when the shots were fired."

He accompanied Jack Considine along the path that led to the tennis courts.

"You walked straight along with Arkwright, you say?"

"I'll tell you when we come to the trees where he stopped to light up," replied Jack.

"Right," replied Anthony. "That's what I want you to."

They walked on. Then Considine stopped and pointed.

"Arkwright fell behind just here and sidled up to that tree for shelter."

Anthony walked to the tree. He looked round. "All in order, Considine," he shouted. "Here's the match he threw away."

He quickly rejoined his companion.

"I don't think I shall have to trouble you for any more information. This time, I propose to show you where you were when you were shot at."

"What do you mean?" Jack Considine stared at him, incredulously.

"Wait a moment. You'll see what I mean."

They walked on for a short distance, Considine watching him curiously. Suddenly Anthony stopped and caught his companion by the arm.

"This is where you were when the first shot was fired. Approximately. Am I right?"

"You are, you wizard," responded Jack. "This is almost the identical spot."

Anthony laughed. "Well, I told you I would, didn't I?"

"Explain yourself, for the love of Mike!"

Anthony shook his head. "All in good time. Believe me, I have an excellent reason for keeping silent—for the present. I am sure you will understand."

"What do you think, Bathurst?" asked Sir Charles Considine when they returned. "Shall I put Baddeley on to it in the morning?"

"As you please, sir—but I don't think he'll be able to help you much."

He turned away to greet Mary who had come up to the group. She spoke to him quietly.

Then I saw him jerk his head up and say, "Certainly! I'll come now!"

They wandered away, and as I watched them, Sir Charles broke out again.

"It's all very well for Bathurst to talk as he does. Baddeley won't be able to help me, indeed! Deuced fine outlook when you can't take a stroll in your own garden without having your brains blown out. What do you think, Bill?"

I turned to reply when a hand touched my sleeve. It was Mary, who had just returned from her walk with Anthony.

She had a curiously strained and excited look on her face.

"Bill," she said, "that question you asked me to-day—so seriously. I've decided to give you the chance you want. You're far too hot for me at cricket, I know that well enough. We'll consider that game played. But I'll play you eighteen holes of golf over at Cranwick to-morrow morning. Jack will caddie for you and Mr. Bathurst has promised to do the same for me. And, Bill, jolly good luck!"

<h1 style="text-align:center">Chapter XXI<br>MR. BATHURST WAVES HIS HAND</h1>

I WENT to bed that night with a feeling of intense exhilaration. Mary's challenge, with anything like ordinary luck, meant a pretty comfortable victory for me, for although only a moderate golfer—my handicap was twelve—the strength and power of my long game should prove too much for Mary whatever she might do with me on the green. And victory for me, according to the Considine Manor tradition, would mean the equivalent of "Yes" to my proposal. For Mary to run the risk of a defeat from me at golf was tantamount to an admission that she loved me. At the same time as I came to consider the matter more fully I began to realize that I shouldn't be able to throw anything away. Mary had the well-merited reputation of winning many a hole by the uncanny accuracy of her short game. As Jack Considine had said to me more than once in the past when discussing his sister's game—"Bill—she's a perfect whale at putts." I came to the conclusion that if I could consistently out-drive her and only keep my head on the green, I should be on velvet as regards the game's ultimate result. When I woke next morning this idea was uppermost in my mind and the brilliant August sun that poured in at my bedroom-window only served to make me even more confident. Mary was a prize worth playing for! I forgot all the recent sinister associations of the Manor and, freshly tubbed and newly razored, floated gaily down to a light but pleasing breakfast.

Anthony was nowhere to be found. He had breakfasted, I heard upon inquiry, very early, and had excused himself to the others, upon an errand of some importance.

Also—there was no sign of Mary. I concluded—without any worrying—that she was taking full time over her matutinal toilet.

The Cranwick course was a matter of half an hour's easy stroll from the Manor so that leaving there at ten o'clock we should be able to make a start very little after half-past ten.

"I've been as good as my word, Bill." Sir Charles bustled into the breakfast room. "I've 'phoned to Baddeley and he's coming along at once. He seems to think that last night's affair has a bearing upon poor Gerry Prescott."

I'm afraid I wasn't as interested as he was or even as I should have been—to me Prescott was dead. Past helping! My mind was of Mary. I muttered a commonplace answer and turned away. Then with an apology I wandered into the garden. When well away from the house, I tried a swing with an imaginary club and thought of all my golfing vices,—those my friends delighted in pointing out. Did I swing too fast?—Did I cut across the ball? Did I "grumph" a straightforward shot? I tried another swing and decided that there was nothing wrong with it. I was full of confidence as I looked at my watch. Time was getting on. I went back to the house, got my clubs, and strolled off towards Cranwick. I should keep my nerve better, I concluded, if I went alone—and the idea came to me that perhaps Mary had given way to the same idea. It was five and twenty minutes past ten when I reached the Cranwick course and the others had already arrived. Jack Considine, looking none the worse for his narrow escape on the previous evening, was talking to his sister when Anthony came forward to meet me.

"Morning, Bill!" he sang out. "Fit and well?" He grinned. "Because you'll need to be, my lad, to win. I've been giving Mary the benefit of some special coaching. Don't see why you should walk away with all the plums."

I laughed. "I'm top-hole, old man—and out to win—take it from me."

As I spoke Mary looked straight across at me. I could see that she was frightfully nervous, and I can tell you I wasn't sorry to see it. She walked over to me—her hands were trembling. As she noticed me glance at them she blushed deliciously and to cover her confusion bent down to tie the lace of her brogue that had come undone. She attempted to put it right—but unsuccessfully—so, looking up at me shyly, called me to fix things for her.

"Are you ready—you two?" cried Anthony—"time's getting on, you know."

"What's your handicap, Mary?" I asked.

She shook her head. "You have the honour, Bill, and please get it over quickly."

I took the first two holes easily—actually doing the second, of 400 yards, in birdie. Mary, on each occasion, finished hopelessly bunkered on the left-hand side of the "fairway." Too confident, possibly, I approached the third somewhat carelessly. It was the shortest hole of the eighteen—135 yards only. I sliced my tee-shot badly and Mary with her best drive of the morning laid herself "dead" on the green. After I had blundered further into the rough she made me one-up only with the most nonchalant of "putts." I was two-up after the fourth but by deadly work on the green Mary took the fifth and sixth. The seventh saw me hook my "tee-shot" most flagrantly but I recovered for a half. I took the eighth, but the ninth—another short hole—went like its fellow, the third, to my opponent. Thus at the turn we were "all square."

"There's no wind, Bill!" exclaimed Anthony—"you ought to be doing better than you are. Keep your head down more and give your hips a bit more freedom. Then you'll win in a canter, laddie." Whether the advice helped me or not I can't say but I went straight away with the tenth and eleventh—both in Bogey. The twelfth and thirteenth were each halved. The fourteenth went to Mary—the fifteenth was halved thanks to a magnificent "putt" by Mary. From a nasty lie, she holed at a distance of six feet and as the ball rattled against the back of the tin, her assurance and sang-froid were amazing. Now the sixteenth was another short hole of 158 yards—Bogey being three. In appearance and general "lie" it was something like the old Harley Street at Woking with its straight menacing lines of gorse and heather that seemed to converge upon the player. Nobody could ever go straight at that hole. But by now I was playing with the genius of inspiration. I did a four and took the hole. With sixteen holes played therefore I was dormy two. As we started for the seventeenth I saw Anthony wave to somebody in the distance. "There's Baddeley," he said. "Suppose there's some news or something. He's coming this way." "Can't help his troubles," I replied as I teed up to lay a lovely shot well past the pin. Mary landed in a pot bunker to the right of the green. I smiled. The game was in my hands. My second shot left me with a two feet "putt." But Mary had the light of battle in her eyes. "Give me my niblick, Mr. Bathurst, will you?" she said very quietly. She went to her ball and with a perfectly wonderful pitch-shot out of the wet sand landed beautifully on to the green along which her ball slowly trickled to hit the back of the tin. I gasped! It was her hole!

"You've not won yet, Bill," she uttered grimly. The last hole was over 400 yards—Bogey four. I took a fine straight drive down the "pritty." Mary on the other hand hooked her tee-shot into the rough and after playing the odd she was still in the rough. She couldn't hope therefore for anything better than a five. I rubbed my hands in unconcealed delight. I could reach the green with a full brassie shot, which was a trifle risky, or I could "kick my hat along" for a five and make absolutely certain of a half at the worst. I determined to be magnificent! "Give me the brassie," I called to Jack. I struck fiercely and quickly—a good enough shot but with just the suspicion of a "pull." To my utter consternation the ball pitched in a small bunker. Mary came well out of the gorse. I was rattled. My recovery was poor and I saw Mary, playing beautifully, get her five and the hole. All square! As her last shot rattled the tin, Baddeley walked up briskly, his face alight with excitement.

"A grand game, Miss Considine. I never felt more excited in all my life than over that last hole. I want you to grant me a favour. Could I have that ball of yours as a memento?" Mary nodded—too overcome to speak and he looked towards me as though in support of his request.

"I'll get it for you, Baddeley," I said and bent down to collect it. As I did so he sprang forward and something clicked on my wrists. I heard Baddeley's voice—faint yet distinct—miles away seemingly!

"William Cunningham, I arrest you for the Wilful Murder of Gerald Prescott and I warn you that anything you may say may be used as evidence against you."

Then Mary fell in a dead faint on the grass.

# CHAPTER XXII
# MR. BATHURST REMINISCENT

I HAVE BEEN asked by Cunningham to write the concluding chapter to the manuscript that has just reached me. Needless to say it has travelled by a somewhat circuitous route from the institution wherein he has been detained for so many years. My presence there in the latter part of last year awakened, no doubt, his egotistical interest in the crime, and caused him to put his own account of it to paper. His accompanying note to me contains the remark that after all I am pre-eminently the right person to finish the affair. Perhaps I am. At any rate, I've decided to do what he requests, if only to stifle certain ill-founded and prejudiced statements that were current for some time after Cunningham's arrest, trial, sentence and subsequent detention "during His Majesty's pleasure." Now for the facts. The great difficulty for us who attempted to investigate the Considine Manor tragedy lay in the separation of the "faked" clues from the true ones. That, of course, to a certain extent, would apply with equal force to a number of other crimes, but in this instance we were arrayed against a criminal—proved afterwards to be a homicidal maniac who had deliberately set out to lead us astray. That was, as I have foreshadowed, our main trouble. Our second difficulty was the apparent absence of motive. But after a time this second matter became less obscure to me. I have read Cunningham's account of the tragedy very carefully, and I will say this: he has been very fair to his readers. Only three clues have been kept from them, and in two of these three cases he himself is unaware of them to this day. The third omission he can be forgiven, for to have given it in its full significance at the time when it came under my notice would have destroyed some of the interest in the narrative from the pure mystery-story point of view. I will now attempt to show how I arrived at my conclusions. When I was called to the billiard room that morning I was very much at sea—the whole thing seemed untrue, but when I pulled my wits together I eventually found that I had to find satisfactory answers to four questions.

(a) Why was Prescott wearing brown shoes?

(b) Why had the dagger been used as well as the lace?

(c) Had Prescott dressed *himself—because his handkerchief was up his right-hand sleeve—and his one laced shoe had been tied in a most peculiar manner—*I only discovered this by actually handling it.

(d) Why was he there—what had brought him?

The question of the handkerchief was unobserved by Cunningham—yet it was the first slip he had made! The lace business he realized, for he spotted me looking at it closely. I will try to describe its peculiarity. The lace of the shoe had been tied in a bow over a reef-knot. I had never seen a lace tied quite like that before, and it was only by an accident I noticed it, for it wasn't exactly obvious to a casual observer. Well, these two facts suggested a train of thought in my mind—had Prescott been murdered—*then* dressed or partially dressed—and *brought* to the billiard room? Had he been brought there from the garden? For there was mud on his shoes but *no mud* on the billiard room floor—despite glaringly obvious signs of a struggle and disturbance! With that idea I paid a visit to Prescott's bedroom. I observed there were nine stairs to be negotiated—not an impossible distance to carry a dead body—for a very powerful man. My idea you see was beginning to take shape. Prescott's bedroom told me something else. While there, I was able to make a deduction of which I am secretly rather proud! It will be remembered that the dressing space of the room was between the entrance-door and the bed, that is to say on the right of a person lying in the bed on his back. Now when a person gets out of bed he invariably turns the bedclothes *away* from the side where he gets out. For example, a person leaving this bed, to dress the side of the entrance-door would undoubtedly fling the clothes away to his *left—yet these clothes were all lying and trailing on the side by the door.* Baddeley took this as evidence that the bed had been slept in—to me it was conclusive evidence in the other direction. I was not concerned for the moment with the missing money. I was reconstructing the crime. The next stage was the garden—the footprints under the billiard room window. For a long time these disconcerted me. There were the four sets and the two kinds. Who had been Prescott's companion? Did Prescott come from the billiard room into the garden? Had he climbed up into the billiard room from the garden? Had the footprints any relation at all to the billiard room? Then the amazing truth hit me. There was no sign of a descent from the billiard room—the earth below was clear. The shoes didn't show a trace of scraping—yet why on earth had Prescott put them on, and not his ordinary dress-shoes? They were on Prescott's feet because the *murderer wished us to see them there*—the footprints were faked—Prescott had not been outside at all—*the murderer had worn them himself.* It was at this stage that Lady Considine's pearls made their appearance or rather their disappearance, and once again the job of unravelling the two skeins presented itself. Just as I had convinced myself they were dissociated from each other, came that startling discovery of the shoe-lace in Webb's pocket. To my mind this was Cunningham's second slip—he managed to get it into the pocket during the struggle that preceded Webb's arrest—but it can be argued that it might very easily have served to hang Webb. I tried hard to persuade myself that Webb must and should be the murderer, but my instinct was always in conflict and I felt that the robbery was just a coincidence. It was hard to place accurately the evidence of the noises in the night—hard, that is, at this stage of the inquiry. I will attempt to explain them later. But so far, I had gone a long way towards sorting out the conditions of the crime, but had found no direct evidence against anybody in particular. But the finding of this shoe-lace opened my eyes a bit, and began to narrow down my field of suspicion. The next point was the discovery of the I.O.U., given to Prescott by Barker. How had that got into the billiard-table pocket? For a long time I was uncertain—then once again the solution came to me. By reason and by memory. It had been put there with deliberation! Nobody had used that room—we *knew*—till Cunningham and I went there—by "used" I mean—played billiards there. The servants gave it a wide berth for transparent reasons. I cast my mind back to the morning Prescott had been discovered—I visualized the entire scene—what had struck me about the "*billiards*" part of it? I had it! The three balls were lying in the pocket near the murdered man's hand—*and the red ball was on top*. The splash of colour it had made against Prescott's white hand had been vivid to me. Yet *when I knocked the balls from the same pocket to commence our game—the spot ball was on top*—they had been moved—surely for the secretion of the Barker I.O.U.— *since the murder*. This caused me to eliminate Barker from my list of "suspects" and I began to grow uneasy. I decided upon that second visit to Prescott's bedroom for I realized I had made a mistake. I hadn't examined the inner apartment. Here I ran across the "stub" of the cigar—my idea had almost become a certainty! Then I began to appreciate the horror of the affair to me—what had come to Bill Cunningham? Yet I clung to the hope that my trail would lead to somebody else at the end, and I dared not let him know what I suspected! Here came Cunningham's third slip! The letter fragments he found were his own. He was getting desperate now and out to involve as many people as he possibly could—why not confuse matters more? He had an old letter from Mary Considine in his letter-case—probably retained for sentimental reasons—written years before and quite inno-cent. "She would meet him somewhere—the station probably—in the 'Bean'—the car they had at the time." He suddenly realized the significance of the time she mentioned in the letter—"faked" it to appear relevant to the murder and "discovered" it under Prescott's bed. I saw through this very quickly—strangely, Mary can't remember ever having written it. Still, I determined to be certain so I popped up to see Mrs. Prescott. Alas! my terrible theory received no shaking. Her son was not ambidextrous and therefore not likely to wear his handkerchief in his wrong sleeve. Also as far as she knew, he was no fancy knot-tier. Running into Baddeley there, was remarkable, and of course he was on a wild-goose chase; Barker and Hornby were merely visiting Mrs. Prescott in the hope that she would accept payment of Lieutenant Barker's debt of honour. He told me this next morning. I made some more investigations that day that revealed the fact to me that Cunningham's grandfather had committed suicide after making a ferocious and entirely uncalled-for attack upon a Roman Catholic priest residing in his neighbourhood. This decided me. Any thought that to arrest Cunningham might savour of treachery towards a friend—was dispelled. I owed it to the community to put him away where he could wreak no more harm and I arrived home that night only to hear of his attack upon Jack. The rest is known. Now this is the matter of the murder! Cunningham's jealousy of Prescott, born of the loss of his Cricket "blue" had been fanned into a blazing flame by the invitation of Prescott for the Considine "week" and his strenuous attentions to Mary. He felt that Prescott intended a proposal and how he hated him for what he called his cursed presumption! Prescott's success during the week and his own failures brought matters to a climax. He'd kill him and he'd also set Anthony Bathurst a nice little problem. He borrowed the shoes from Prescott's bedroom immediately after dinner, and when the others first adjourned to the drawing-room he constructed the "footprints," returned the shoes and kept one of the laces. He intended to hide in the inner bedroom before Prescott came to bed and then strangle him from behind by taking him unawares. Things went well for him—he saw Barker's I.O.U. passed over and noted it. Also he noticed Hornby fingering the Venetian dagger, so he removed that—wearing gloves—when he went up to bed—it had Hornby's finger-prints—and also might be useful if it came to a "rough house" with Prescott. Against this, however, Dennis had seen him in the garden—without, of course, recognizing him, and Mary had been conscious of the "espionage" that was connected with the "smell of a cigar." As a matter of fact his jealousy had caused him to follow Prescott and Mary several times before—as she told us. Arrived in Prescott's bedroom he sought a hiding-place in the bathroom, and was there when Barker went along to bed. When the latter was being questioned by Baddeley as to the people that were upstairs when he went to bed, Cunningham stated that he answered Barker's "good-night." He did *not*, because *he was in Prescott's bedroom and not in his own*. When Prescott came to bed he naturally began to undress—probably sitting on the bed with his back towards Cunningham. Waiting for a favourable opportunity the latter sprang on his victim and strangled him with the lace—leaving a cigar stub in the inner room. His fourth mistake!

Prescott, no doubt, had previously removed his coat, vest, tie, collar and shoes. In the struggle the bed-clothes were disarranged, and subsequently pushed on to the floor by Cunningham.

He then abstracted Barker's I.O.U. and collected all Prescott's spare cash. All he had to do now was to dress Prescott again—which he did, making the two mistakes alluded to—wait till the whole house was quiet—and then carry him downstairs to the billiard room—the brown shoes of course being used for the purpose that I have shown to give the affair an "outside" connection. Everybody was asleep, and he probably went in his stockinged feet—it was a thousand to one nobody would hear him. But Jack Considine heard him shut his own bedroom door upon his return. Whitney, the motorist, saw the light go up in the billiard room when Cunningham entered with his ghastly burden—but that was all he could see. Cunningham probably wore gloves all the time—there were no finger-marks. But he knew that Major Hornby's finger-marks would show on the dagger which he had had no occasion to use. So he used it—driving it into Prescott's dead body. It would cause the police much mystification, and throw suspicion on Hornby.

The noises that Arkwright and his wife heard were consequent upon the visit of the "Spider"—about an hour after the actual murder and say an hour or so before the descent to the billiard room. The attack on Jack Considine I can only attempt to explain. But my conjecture is that Cunningham's jealousy had reached such extreme limits that he was infuriated by Jack's praise of Prescott at breakfast that morning. He used the lumber shed to fire from—that was how I told Jack the exact spot of the outrage. He had used the shed before to hide behind when following Mary and Prescott. Even then I made him convict himself—I felt that I must remove all shred of doubt before telling Sir Charles and getting Baddeley to act. I arranged with Mary to play Cunningham the eighteen holes of golf—fearing the possible consequences of a refusal on her part as he was by that time in a dangerous state. I arranged for her shoe-lace to come undone—and that she should get Cunningham to tie it for her. He was excited—he forgot himself—*he tied it exactly as he had tied Prescott's shoe*! I had arranged with Baddeley to give him the signal if my worst fears were confirmed. I did so. When the time came we acted quickly.

I try to forget it all—and now, having written this account of it, am going to try all the harder. For then I can think of him as he was before that dreadful madness turned his brain, and after all—

"There—but for the Grace of God—goes—any one of us!"

THE END

# AFTERWORD

If you haven't finished the book, do go back and read it before reading this, as there is something that should be discussed.

There has been a concern that Flynn, in his first attempt at writing crime fiction, copied a central idea from a highly successful book from the previous year – fans of the Golden Age will know which book I refer to, but I will not name it here for fear of spoilers. This is actually not so; it is simply the case of two similar ideas being developed in parallel, independent of each other. The manuscript for *The Billiard-Room Mystery* took some time to be picked up for publication by John Hamilton and indeed was left half-finished for at least six months in a drawer. He simply would not have had enough time to re-write it enough to copy that other book's idea. The plot came entirely from Flynn desiring to write something original. It's also worth pointing out the most famous use of this trick was also not the first instance, with at least three earlier works employing it.

Interestingly, the comparison never seems to have been made in newspaper reviews at the time. We should give Flynn the benefit of any doubt that might linger.

Steve Barge

Printed in Great Britain
by Amazon

79381988R10108